On Midnight Ridge

B. J. Ray

October, 2000
Herefordshire

Tears of grief streamed down Jenny Montfort's cheeks, as she walked westward on the springy, sheep-nibbled grass of Midnight Ridge - a wild, hilltop place. A cutting breeze swept through the gorse and the dying ferns, in the valley below, forgotten bales of straw lay in stubble fields, and the air was heavy with the smell of cut hedges. Autumn was pushing summer from the hills, and from the hazel-lined drover's road which led to the ridge; shorter days and long shadows pointed toward winter.

On reaching Martha's Tump, high above Earlsbrook village, Jenny sat on the same rock where she had once played Queen of the Castle as a child. She saw her mother's young face, smiling at her, and her words echoing down through the years: "Be careful, Jenny: you'll fall!"

In the churchyard below, family wreaths piled on fresh soil were the only colour, in a valley of green. No tears had come when her mother died, or at her funeral – but now, sitting alone on her childhood rock, she sobbed. The tears were of grief, yes, but also of relief, at last, that it was all over. Never again would that walking stick bang on the bedroom floor, or those harsh words tumble down the stairs.

The love she had felt for her mother, as a child, had faded through adolescence. Everything she had done as a teenager was regarded with suspicion, jealousy or hostility, which had continued into adulthood. Caring had been a call of duty, not love.

Jenny was now forty years old, and all she had ever known was the non-stop rolling of the seasons at Poplar Farm. She felt that the days of her life had passed like the rapidly flicked pages of a book, with little written on them. Now that freedom beckoned, her mind was a tangled mass of briers, pulling in all directions. The livestock would have to go, of that she was sure; no more pulling ewes from drifting snow, in a biting, January wind, or thawing the farmyard tap with kettles of boiling water. For the last time, she had slithered her way to the lambing shed on black-icy, rat-scampering, owl screeching, finger-numbing nights. And, now the tears of grief continued to flow.

"I'm free at last!" She breathed the words into the wind.

As she walked the stone-walled track, back down to the village, clouds of bees and wasps, who were gorging on the autumnal crop of ivy flower nectar, flew upward, settling again after she passed. A whirling storm of Jackdaws flew overhead, ink-blots against the blue; muscle, sinew, bone and feather synchronized them in perfect, fan-shaped symmetry – then, they were gone.

Jenny opened the farmhouse door and stared into the silent, dimly-lit kitchen. A flypaper, covered in corpses, hung above the kitchen table; beside it, a dusty, cobwebbed card read: *"Hereford Fat-Stock Market - Best Pen of Lambs, 1984"*. Maggie, the family cat, was sleeping peacefully on a pile of her mother's clothes, which were airing on the plate-rack above the kitchen stove. Two holes, worn in the tablecloth by her father's elbows, were the only evidence left of him having eaten his way through sixty summers at Poplar Farm. Every time Jenny had tried to get rid of it, her mother had said: "Leave it, in case 'e comes in fer 'is dinner again!" So, the tablecloth stayed: a permanent memorial to a rustic life gone. She took the flypaper down, pulled the cloth from the table and binned them both, saying: "Sorry, Dad."

Taking the card down from the beam, she recalled Tommy, her first boyfriend; a drover at Hereford cattle market. When her mother had discovered why Jenny was so keen to go with her father to market each week, a phone call to Tommy's parents had ended it. Whenever boys became attentive, Jenny had always blamed herself when they lost interest: perhaps she was not pretty enough; too young; too old; too fast or too slow? Then, one day, she overheard the telephone conversation, as her mother was berating her latest: "Don't you come 'ere again. I know a lot about your father; we don't need your sort 'ere!"

If a phone call didn't work, guilt was the other tool in her mother's armoury. "Yer dad needs you here, now he's gettin' older!" was her favourite phrase. Or, maybe: "Who's going to help yer dad lambing, if you're off galavantin'?"

Getting rid of the tablecloth and the card was her first, tentative step in moving from past to present, and to her newfound freedom. Now was *her* time.

November, 2000

The auctioneer's gavel tapped away the lots and minutes of farm-sale day, as heads nodded, sticks waved and eyes winked. Every time it hit the rostrum, another piece of Jenny's family life became someone else's property; pens of sheep, hurdles, buckets, a root-pulper, pitchforks, axes, scythes, a hedging slash, sickles, shovels, corn bins, old Tilley lamps covered in dust, small hay bales, rusty gates, rolls of wire, corrugated iron, chicken coops, chains, an old horse harness: all were bundled into vans and trailers, to leave her life forever.

Phoebe and Henry Dunhill-Smith, from Court Farm, were standing behind the bidders. Jenny knew they were not here to buy, but to be nosy, and to gloat at the ending of her farming life, while theirs was in the ascendency.

Jenny watched as the auctioneer's assistant held up her father's billhook and heavy, leather hedging mitt.

"Lot 143, gentlemen. What am I bid?"

Jenny saw the handle, polished by the sweat of her father's hand, and pictured him pleaching hawthorn and holly, as he laid them into stock-proof hedges.

"No, no, no; not them!" she shouted, running through the throng of bidders. She grabbed them and headed for the sanctuary of the farm's kitchen. Phoebe Dunhill-Smith smirked, but did not speak as she passed.

Jenny slammed the door, shutting out the noise of the auction and the image of Phoebe's face, enjoying the sight of her emotions on public display. Fondling the billhook handle, she thrust her nose into the hedging mitt and inhaled the last vestiges of her father's presence on Earth. She smelt comfort, security, happiness, sadness, bonfire smoke, childhood, adolescence and laughter. She saw his ageing hands, too weak to handle a cup; hands which were once strong enough to catch a running sheep by its fleece and bring it down for shearing; strong enough to lift the leg of an unwilling bullock, to tend a wound, yet gentle enough to pull a lamb from its mother's womb.

When he succumbed to the passage of too many sunsets, her mother became even more hurtful, making Jenny's life a misery. A farming-family's life, which had once seemed endless, closed.

*

She awoke to the sad silence of a farm with no livestock, and a stillness so thick you could slice it. Through the kitchen window, Jenny could see three chickens, a cockerel, a goose and two feral pigeons, stood on top of a grass bank, peering forlornly in at her. Her pregnant mare, Trudy, was grazing in the orchard, underneath the old pear tree. These were the only animals left, after three generations of Montforts had toiled, tilled, harvested and sweated the seasons and decades away, at Poplar Farm.

She threw some crusts and a bowl of corn out to them and switched on the radio. The weather forecast said remnants of a hurricane were about to cross the country, at lunchtime. She loved Midnight Ridge in any weather, but it was spectacular in a storm - Jenny felt the urge to go there again, to let the elements blow away her sorrow.

Striding head-on into the wind, each step was a battle. The north-westerly tore at her clothes, in an ear-roaring, tear-inducing, cold-cheeked celebration of weather at its wildest. She could see the crest above the old quarry; the moorland ponies, silhouetted against the skyline; and sheep scattered like flotsam, across the dying moorland ferns. She headed for the five pine trees, huddled together for comfort on the old drover's trail, and knew from stormy days past that there would be a pool of silence and tranquillity on the lea-ward side of the trees - her own private, open-air cathedral.

Behind her, to the south, the sun shone. To the north, an enormous, black storm cloud billowed and rolled its way over the mountains and valleys of Wales.

The first stinging raindrop hit as she reached the oasis of calm. She leant her back against a tree trunk to gather breath, and stared in wonderment at the wild sky, as it closed in.

"You must be as mad as I am, to be up here in this!" The man's voice startled her.

Jenny turned to see a tall figure, leaning against the tree next to her, and was momentarily angry that anyone else should have invaded her private pool of silence, as she watched her storm. She had no words to reply with, so simply stood watching the gale vent its fury on the hills, saying nothing. Stray pieces of bracken came rolling in front of the gathering wind, and a shower of pine needles streamed eastward, dancing on the breeze. The sheep and ponies had their rumps windward, as they grazed.

That she was not alone gave Jenny an uneasy feeling that she had never known before. She had always felt at one with the hills, and part of the landscape - like a stone in one of the wandering walls. The only times she ever knew real loneliness was in a crowd, or on the few occasions she had visited a city. Never on Midnight Ridge, even in darkness.

A rogue gust of wind forced a single raven to ground, right in front of her. It stopped momentarily, croaked like a frog when it saw her, then took off again, lifting high into the air, without a single flap of its wings. She heard her mother's voice, saying: "Ravens carry the souls of the dead to Heaven."

"Why, Mother, why?" she said, without thinking.

The stranger turned toward her, showing his face for the first time. "Are you okay?"

"Yes... thank you. But, I came here to be alone." Jenny regretted the words as soon as she had said them.

"I'm sorry: I didn't mean to invade your privacy," the stranger said, before turning and walking away, into the rain, with head down.

She watched his silhouette, growing smaller and fainter, as the storm closed in, wondering who he was and why he was there. Her only recollection of his face was his incredible blue eyes, amid the greyness of the storm. She wanted to call after him, to apologize, but she knew her words would blow away, like discarded feathers.

December, 2000

Jacob Adams made a cup of unsweetened, black coffee, covered two rounds of toast in butter and sat staring at his computer, yet he couldn't bring himself to switch it on; motivation to work was harder with every day that passed. The deadline for the programme he was writing was approaching like a peregrine falcon in full stoop.

He sipped his coffee, staring at the blank screen, his thoughts wandering. He was forty-six and work had been his life; a lucrative niche in the computer industry had provided him with everything he needed, except the time to settle down. Now, middle age was pointing its wrinkled finger at him. Financial success meant he could afford to retire, which was a great comfort, but somehow not quite the pinnacle of achievement he had always thought it would be.

He had spent most of his working days in London, Birmingham and cities all across Europe. To escape from the desk, he walked or cycled around wherever he happened to be at the time.

For total isolation, he hid himself away in his beloved cottage, left to him by his grandfather, in the Welsh Marches. Here, he rode his mountain bike through forests heavy with the smell of pine, walked hills free of traffic fumes and gazed at unpolluted night skies. It was on Midnight Ridge that he saw his first red kite, soaring over the Welsh hills - a brief, momentary encounter with the truly wild, which changed his view on life. The solitary bird circled, dived, wheeled and, at times, appeared glued to the sky, as it hung motionless on rising thermals. He was at once envious of the raptor's freedom. School, college, university and work had absorbed his days, like dry sand takes in water, and the flight of the kite lifted him above this world; for the first time, he saw a man in an uncaring, ruthless and cut-throat city, chained to a desk, staring at a computer screen. An unfulfilled man, with all the trappings of success, but happiness was somewhere over the horizon, untouchable and out of reach. As the months passed, the thoughts took root, in the deepest recesses of his mind. For the first time in his life, he was unsure what to do with his future.

He returned to the present and his mirror image in the greyness of the laptop screen. The decision was made: from this moment forward, he would never turn a computer on again.

His mobile phone rang, dragging him back to reality.

"Eric Jackson here, Jake. Just wondered when the program will be finished. The boss wants it like, err, yesterday, pal!"

"Tell the boss it's not finished, and never will be... pal: I've just retired!" Jacob pressed the "end" button and ended his career.

*

As he drove up the valley toward Quarry Cottage, a crimson sunset burnt its way into the blackness of the trees of Sheepcratch Hill. The pine trees on Midnight Ridge stood against the skyline, like arrows pointing to Heaven. To the east side of the cottage, a busy squirrel buried mast for winter, under the leafless skeleton of his beech-tree home.

After unloading his bags from the car, Jacob poured a large Welsh whisky, lit the log burner and loaded it with oak blocks. Switching on his C.D. player, he settled into his grandfather's leather armchair, closed his eyes and drifted lazily in a summer sky - like the kite - as he listened to Vaughan Williams: "The Lark Ascending".

He drained the whisky glass and climbed the crooked elm staircase to bed. A tawny owl hooted from the beech tree, as sleep overtook him.

Christmas Eve, 2000

Jacob looked out of his bedroom window. A hard frost covered the hills white, like fine sugar sprinkled from a sieve. A low sunrise was melting crystallized grass blades, etching shadow of trees and fence posts, green on white. On top of the churchyard wall, alongside Quarry Cottage, a pair of jackdaws preened each other like lovers, both relishing the early-morning warmth.

Feeling slightly hungover, Jacob drank a large mug of strong, black coffee and left the cottage to talk to his grandfather. Five generations of his family were buried in St. John's Churchyard, next to the cottage. He opened the lychgate and walked between rows of lichen-encrusted tombstones, stopping before his great-grandfather's, to read the inscription, which he knew by heart:

> *To the memory of Jacob Elijah Adams*
> *Who died November 21ˢᵗ 1904.*
>
> *"To you who do my grave pass by*
> *As you are now, so once was I*
> *As I am now, so you must be*
> *Prepare in time to follow me..."*

He walked on, on foot-crunching grass, along the rows of graves, stopping before his grandfather's. Here was the resting place of David Adams, the only man with whom Jacob had ever had a deep, personal understanding; the man who gave him his love of nature. His parents had moved away from Earlsbrook, before he was born, and were too career-conscious to spend any time with him during school holidays. So, these were his formative days - his Grandad days - spent trout fishing; bird-nesting; fire lighting; bow, arrow and stick-making, for hours, followed by nights star-reading, from the cottage window.

"I've done it, Grandad. I said I would!"

The silence which followed was interrupted by the piercing shrill of a robin claiming territorial rights.

"I've finished. No more city days; no more computer. I'm back here, with you."

The robin flew down and perched on the next gravestone. He looked at Jacob intently, tilting his head from side to side, the sunlight igniting his breast like burning coal.

"Hello, robin," Jacob said. "I'm talking to Grandad." The bird was now less than two feet from him, answering back with a low, chuckling conversation, his throat feathers moving as he spoke. Avian and human worlds became one, as they talked to each other in the velvet silence of the churchyard. The inquisitive bird gave another ear-piercing trill, then was gone. Jacob felt moved by the encounter, as if the rufous-breasted songster knew he was at a life-changing juncture, and had come to give approval.

"Grandad, I'm going up on the ridge now, for a bike ride. I'll meet you at our vantage point, by the stream!" He wiped a tear from his eye.

As he turned to leave, Jacob noticed a recent grave without a headstone. On the bare soil, a temporary undertaker's plaque read: *"Alice Montfort"*. Beside it lay a bunch of holly, mistletoe and bare twigs, with a card attached. He stooped to read the message:

> *"Spindle, holly and mistletoe.*
> *For the memory of childhood walks,*
> *hedgerows, hayricks and happier days. Why,*
> *Mother, why?*
> *Jenny."*

The words elevated Jacob back to Midnight Ridge, and the memory of the woman who had come to the pine trees, out of the storm. Why had she said those words - *"Why, Mother, why?"* - as the raven landed? He recalled feeling a sense of guilt, as he had walked away, leaving her alone in the snarling teeth of a storm, wondering whether to turn back and see her safely down from the hilltop.

But, his overpowering recollection was one of exhilaration, at the incredible skyscape: broad rays of sunlight, amid dark, racing clouds; a magnificent natural drama, in the natural amphitheatre between Midnight Ridge and Sheepcratch Hill.

*

Jacob's legs ached with exertion, as he reached the plateau at the western end of Midnight Ridge. Loose stone, icy patches, broken branches and ruts caused by stormwater made the steep ride - from Quarry Cottage to the trig point, on Midnight Ridge - a heart-thumping challenge. His lungs were on fire and steam drifted downwind, from his sweat-soaked cycling top. He leant his mountain bike against a lichen-covered rock.

After a few breath-catching moments, the effects of the climb dissipated, to become a heady feeling of elation. Walking over to the stream he had camped by with his grandad, many times, he knelt down, scooped ice-cold water in his hands and plunged his face into it. Childhood returned, for a fleeting second.

Refreshed, he stood, hung his binoculars around his neck and walked to the plateau's edge. Scree tumbled down to the valley floor, and at eye-level a kestrel was pinned to the sky - head down, weight cradled on air currents, as it rose effortlessly up the rock-strewn escarpment; only the quivering tail feathers, adjusting to maintain position on the breeze, gave any hint that this was a living being. The hawk's eyes scanned the rugged terrain for prey, then a sudden, bullet-nosed dive ended in a talon-pierced vole being carried high above Jacob. He watched through his binoculars as the tiny mammal struggled hopelessly, on its way to the raptor's feeding post. Two tiny specks of blood appeared on the lens of Jacob's field glasses, as the kestrel winged out of sight: a full-colour reminder that raw nature is even more ruthless and brutal than the city life he had just left behind.

*

Jenny was facing her first Christmas alone at Poplar Farm.

Mole, her father's faithful farmworker, for fifty-one years, was carrying a basket of oak logs to the house, as she went out to start her battered, old 4x4. "It's Christmas tomorrow, missus," he said, trudging across the slippery yard.

Jenny slammed the vehicle door, so he couldn't hear her reply: "Thanks for stating the bloody obvious, Mole!"

In the weeks of mourning since her mother's funeral, Jenny had kept herself busy, clearing up paperwork from the farm and reorganizing the house. She had considered selling up, many times, but felt that she needed the security of the only home she had ever known. Having no stock to tend had left a void, which she now had no idea how to fill, so she had taken to going up to the common which straddled Midnight Ridge every day, to check on her neighbour Seb Morris's sheep, watch the wild ponies and walk. The beauty of ever-changing skies freed her mind, giving her time and space to muse upon her newfound freedom, and how to use it. She couldn't ride Trudy, her chestnut horse, up to the ridge at the moment, because she was heavy with foal.

The engine fired up, in a cloud of smoke, and Jenny started the long, steep drive on the drover's road, worn deep into the hillside over centuries, by countless hooves crossing the ridge. Ice-encrusted bones of hawthorn and hazel arched over the track, creating a crystal tunnel, and a magical shower of hoar fell from them, as Jenny drove beneath. Rounding the last bend before the top, a full-face sun filled the sky, temporarily blinding her vision.

Jacob Adams saw the vehicle approach and grabbed at his brake levers, locking both wheels - on the steep, ice-covered surface, this only increased his speed. His bike struck the car's front bumper, head on.

The momentum catapulted him through the air, onto the canvas hood, his weight tearing through the canopy. He landed on a half-used bale of hay, behind the driver's seat.

Jenny thought that a tree branch had fallen through the roof, until she saw a black, lycra-clad human leg, hanging over the back of the passenger seat. Her heart pounded as she stared at the leg, afraid to turn around. "Oh, my god!" she said, as the leg moved.

Opening the driver's door, she ran around to open the tailgate.

Jacob's cycle helmet was rammed down over one ear; a graze above his eye was covered in hay seeds.

"Where the hell did you come from?" she said, not knowing if he was conscious, or even alive.

Two blue eyes looked back at her, in shocked silence, until Jacob recovered enough composure to try and move. After retrieving his leg from the back of the seat, he tried to sit up, as Jenny stood speechless, not knowing how he got there, or what to do now. Jacob realized that nothing was broken, and moved to sit with his legs out of the back of the vehicle. Then, he burst out laughing with relief.

"I'm bloody glad *you* find it funny; I thought I'd killed you!" Jenny shouted. Her attitude only made him laugh more. Then, she began to see the funny side, too, and they laughed together.

*

Jenny parked the truck outside Quarry Cottage and helped Jacob unload his twisted bike.

"One wrecked bike-wheel, a dented ego, and no broken bones!" Jacob said, opening the cottage gate. "Can I offer you a coffee?"

"Perhaps I should introduce myself first: Jenny Montfort, from Poplar Farm, on the opposite side of the ridge."

"Yes, yes, of course... err, Jacob: Jacob Adams. Sorry about the dramatic introduction. Now, will you have that coffee?"

Jenny removed her dung-encrusted Wellington boots at the cottage door, and sat down at the kitchen table. Then, she saw herself in a mirror: dirty, green boiler suit; hair pinned in a bun, underneath her father's old, greasy work cap; torn wax jacket; and heels exposed, through gaping holes in her socks. "Just look at the state of me! I'm surprised you didn't run in the house and slam the door shut!"

Jacob removed his cycle helmet. His black and yellow cycling gear looked as though he had hit a flying farmyard.

There was a silence, as the two strangers, suddenly forced together by circumstance, struggled to know which way to take the conversation. Jacob started making the coffee.

"I found myself laughing for the first time in months, after the accident," Jenny said, to break the silence. "It came as a bit of a surprise... I've been caring for my mother, then she died and I'd almost forgotten how to. I'm just sorry it came at the cost of your downfall."

"Well, if I'm too stupid to realize you can't ride a bike downhill and stop dead on an icy surface, and that made you laugh, that's about the greatest achievement I've had in several months."

Jenny then asked the question which had been on her lips from the moment she saw his blue eyes, looking at her from the back of the truck: "You weren't on the ridge a few weeks ago, in a storm, were you?"

Jacob looked at her for a long time, considering his reply. "Yes... and I saw the raven, too. I felt guilty leaving you alone in the storm... but, I guessed you needed the space."

"Oh, the raven... Mother was very superstitious..." Jenny went quiet.

Jacob opened the log-burner door and threw in a log, to

fill a gap in the conversation.

"I was rude to you when we spoke in the storm and I've tried to kill you on the ridge today - quite an introduction, heh? Yet, you're still talking to me!" Jenny smiled.

"Yes. I've had quite a day so far: sworn at by a robin, for trespassing; talked to my long-dead grandfather; watched a vole give his life to a kestrel; taught myself to fly and then crash-landed. And, the townies say not much happens in the countryside!"

Jenny was deep in thought as she sipped her coffee. "This might sound really silly, coming from a stranger, but I'm eating Christmas dinner alone tomorrow, for the first time in my life, and dreading it. I don't suppose you would like to join me?"

"Christmas!? It's Christmas day tomorrow! I've been so wrapped up in my own world, for the last few days, I hadn't even considered Christmas. I've no wife, no kids, and no parents; I usually stay in bed late, have a bacon sandwich, then go out on my bike. Now, I haven't even got a bloody bike!

"So, yes; why not? Thank you."

Christmas Day, 2000

From his bed, Jacob looked out to see a low mist blanketing St. John's Churchyard. A brilliant orange sunrise backlit the shingled spire, piercing the murk; the newly-gilded weather-vane glinted in morning light. The nave and chancel were out of sight, somewhere in the gloom, far below.

He breakfasted on muesli and black coffee. His bike was out of action, so he decided to walk the two miles to Poplar Farm, across the ridge. He left the cottage, mid-morning, walking into the sun. As he climbed the stile leading to a patch of open heath, rising steeply to the ridge, he stopped to listen to the soft silence which only comes on Christmas morning: no vehicles; no birdsong; no sheep or cattle; no children playing; no human voices - the only sound was his heartbeat. Tall columns of smoke, from cottage fires, towered skyward in the still, morning air, levelling out in a blue haze, which followed the contours of the hills.

A pair of red kites came gliding into view, as he crossed a small, concrete bridge, up the track to Poplar Farm. At the entrance to the yard, a huge bannut tree stood, with bare branches reaching out toward a stone barn. Beside the barn, a chattering rookery hinted that spring was near. Below, a bank of snowdrop buds greened the muddy earth.

Mole stood in the barn's doorway, eyeing the stranger suspiciously. As Jacob neared, he shrunk back into the darkness of the cider house, trying - and failing - to be inconspicuous. Still, Jacob pretended not to see him. The hinges of the garden gate squeaked as Jacob opened it, alerting a goose grazing on the lawn that they had a visitor; with gaping beak and outstretched wings it ran, hissing at Jacob. Never having encountered an angry goose before, he backed out of the gate and ran - the wild-eyed bird followed him across the yard.

Mole emerged from the cider house, grinning. He was wearing an oversized boiler suit, a greasy cap and Wellington boots, with the tops turned down.

"Eric wunna 'urt ya. Kick 'im up th'arse!" he said, sinking his boot into the gander's inflated plumage. Eric gave out a loud *"quarrwk"* and gave up the chase, with a defiant shiver of his tail feathers. Ego well satisfied that he had seen off the stranger, he started pulling on grass growing alongside the barn.

"Thank you," Jacob said, keeping well away from Eric, as he made his way to the house. Mole grinned, showing a wide expanse of gums, occupied by a single, brown, tombstone tooth.

Jenny came out of the back door. "Oh, dear. I see you've met Eric - his squawk is far worse than his peck. Sorry I didn't warn you about him. You're very punctual; I expect everyone around here to be late." She held out her hand in welcome.

The farmhouse was built into the lower slopes of Midnight Ridge, in a commanding position. They entered by the back door, into a gloomy kitchen, with a small window looking out at ground level, toward an orchard.

A horse was lying by a hay rack, with chickens and a cockerel scratching around. "That's Trudy, my best friend," Jenny said, as Jacob took in the surroundings. "She's lonely since the cattle went, but she'll soon have her foal to keep her busy. Anyway, welcome to Poplar Farm. Can I offer you some mulled cider, my father's favourite Christmas tipple?"

"Never having tasted mulled cider, I'll try anything once. Yes, thank you."

Jenny lifted the lid of a saucepan, simmering on the stove. The scent of cinnamon filled the kitchen, as she filled two glasses.

"Cheers, and wishing you a non-eventful, peaceful day."

"To health and safety on Midnight Ridge," Jacob said, smiling and raising his glass. "Wow, that's a proper drink!"

"My father's recipe: cider brewed from our own apples, with a splash of whisky and spices. Please, sit down."

Jenny felt a nervousness that she had only ever felt on odd occasions before - like entering a room full of strangers. Jacob was taken aback by her appearance: this was a totally different woman sitting opposite him to yesterday's rustic farmer. Her neat, brunette hair was shoulder-length, with a natural, grey streak, above her deep-brown eyes. She had open, attractive features, with lightly tanned skin and the ruddy cheeks of a life spent outdoors. She was wearing a cream blouse and tweed skirt.

"Thank goodness your labourer was there to save me from Eric," Jacob said, making light conversation.

"Mole? He's part of the farm's fabric. His mother died having him, in the cottage where he still lives. His father died when he was a teenager, and my father took him under his wing. In days gone by he would have been known as backward - the village idiot; not quite the full shilling, as they say. He has two loves in his life: money and our barn. But, he is actually no one's fool, and all the villagers know him for what he is: kind-hearted and wonderful with animals. He may love money, but he is never seen spending it; I expect he'll die a rich man. He lives alone in the cottage, surrounded by trees and undergrowth, and sleeps in our barn more than he does at home. He spends all his days cutting wood for the fires, tending the animals and maintenance chores around the farm. He adored Father and has never taken a penny in wages. He always appears at mealtimes, but always goes out to the cider house to eat."

"Why is he called Mole?"

"His real name is Samuel Gillion. The story goes that when he was at school, in the early fifties, his headmaster told him that he was so thick, all he was any good for was shovelling soil - from that day on he's been known as Mole! Life was tough at school in those days. But, he's muddled through on his own, and knows an animal is sick before I do. He's very sensitive and easily upset.

"Anyway, enough of Mole. Thank you for saving me from eating alone. After my mother died, in October, I was dreading today. I also felt terrible about not seeing you in the blinding sun yesterday, and hope that this will somehow right a wrong."

"It's my pleasure; it seems that we're both at a crossroads. And, I probably know more about you than you realize: I was in the graveyard, telling Grandad about my decision to close my business, when I saw a fresh grave - I guessed it was your mother's, having seen the raven land and hearing your words, then seeing them repeated on the bunch of spindle. You confirmed my suspicions yesterday, when we spoke after the accident."

"My god! You must be David Adams's grandson. Why

didn't I make the link yesterday? Your cottage was let to holidaymakers for years, wasn't it?"

"Yes. I was busy working and only came down occasionally, when it was empty. Did you know my grandfather?"

"No, but my father talked about him many times. They used to meet on the ridge, when Dad was checking the cattle and David was out birdwatching. He told tales about his army days, the war and youthful exploits: bird-nesting, fishing, camping... My father never went to war because of the farm."

Jenny turned to the cooker: "You're here for lunch; I'd better get on with it." She opened the oven door and brought out a roasted chicken. "It's all ready. We're eating in the dining room - the first time it's been used for five years!"

Jacob helped her carry the dishes through to a mahogany table, large enough to seat twelve. Two place settings were laid at one end, with antique silver cutlery and a posy of snowdrop buds. Jacob was used to eating alone, and found the surroundings and circumstances surreal, but the smell of the food spiked his appetite.

"Would you carve? Father always did, and I can't bring myself to do it."

As Jacob lifted the knife to carve, the dining room door burst open. Mole stood in the doorway, looking flustered. "'Er's 'avin' the foal, missus; yer'd better come!"

Jenny said: "Oh, shit! I can't believe this: I checked her this morning and thought she was several days away! I'm awfully sorry. You carry on and have your lunch."

"Not likely! I've never seen an animal born – or, come to that, a human being - and I'd love to watch, if you don't mind."

Trudy was lying by the hay rack, with a membrane-covered hoof protruding from her. Chickens were pecking and scratching in the straw around her.

"I don't know whether to leave her here or try and get her to the stable," Jenny said.

"It's 'er first lickle un; best leave 'er alone," Mole said, with calm confidence. He walked over to the barn and came back with a bale of straw, hanging from the tines of a pitchfork, slung over his shoulder. He walked very slowly around behind Trudy and spread the straw, with all the loving care of a father decorating a nursery for his first-born. Trudy whinnied, as though thanking him for his thoughtfulness. She was sweating around her neck and very restless, standing up and lying down again, several times, with strong and regular contractions.

Jenny, Mole and Jacob stood silently, leaning on the field gate, watching. Then, after an hour of labour, the newborn slithered quietly into Christmas - a steaming, struggling pile of angular bones.

Still covered in placenta, the foal was shaking its head. Mole opened the gate, walked over and ripped the membrane, clearing the foal's nostrils with his finger - its first breath of Earlsbrook air came. After a few minutes, Trudy stood up, whinnied and started licking and pulling at the placenta, while the foal shook its head, in disbelief at its arrival in a strange world.

Jenny turned toward Jacob, smiling.

Tears were streaming down Jacob's cheeks. Nothing he had ever experienced had prepared him for this moment; the cut-throat world of e-commerce had taught him how to handle most situations, but never anything like this. "Thank you! Thank you for letting me share this with you! I have never been so moved in my life! I've seen a new life created! Never before have I seen anything so wonderful!" He turned to Jenny and hugged her, unashamed of his flowing tears.

Mole grinned and said: "It's a lickle stallion, missus."

Jacob and Jenny started back toward the house, leaving Mole watching the newborn and mother. As they approached the gable end of the cider house, a barn owl winged onto the breeze, from a hole in the stonework, into the fading, afternoon light. Jacob stopped to watch it.

"That's Claud - the other resident of the barn, besides Mole," Jenny said.

The owl flew along a low hawthorn hedge, which bounded the orchard, slowing to hover above a tussock of grass, as he flapped his wings and lowered his head, his eyes searching. Then, like a giant phantom butterfly, he flew off into the gathering dusk.

Jenny was smiling to herself as she pulled the chicken, three tureens of shrivelled vegetables and a jug of congealed gravy from the oven. "Welcome to Christmas lunch - now dinner - Poplar Farm-style!" Wisps of smoke rose from the cremated chicken. "I think it's time we had a sherry!"

After the meal, Jacob sat in an armchair which seemed to grow out of the bare, flagstone floor, beside a huge inglenook fireplace. The arms were worn through to the wood, and polished shiny by decades of use. An applewood fire blazed in a large, wrought-iron fire-basket, with a cast-iron kettle hanging from a sway; steam drifted lazily from the spout, disappearing into the gaping blackness of the lounge's chimney. Jacob felt as though he was dreaming a part in some Dickensian play.

Jenny stared into the fire in silence, watching her father's face dance in the flames. "It's so good to see someone sitting in

Father's armchair again. We only ever lit this fire on Christmas day - this is the first time since he died," she said, wistfully.

"When I was a kid, we used to play I Spy, then Mother would play the piano, while Father snored in the chair and I played with my presents. Childhood seemed so long then; now, it seems like a fleeting day. This farm has absorbed my life."

Jacob replied: "This reminds me of campfires with Grandad, when I was a boy; I've never seen a kettle boiling over a fire since then. He taught me about the stars: the Plough, Ursa Major and how to find Polaris, the north star. Orion the hunter; Cygnus the swan; Andromeda... Spending so much time in the city, I've forgotten what a star looks like; light pollution kills stars."

The grandfather clock standing in the hallway struck nine, reminding Jacob that he had yet to walk home. He leant forward in the chair, as if to go: "I'd better think about moving myself."

"I'll drive you home," Jenny said, as Jacob rose reluctantly from the armchair.

"No, honestly, I love walking the ridge in darkness. With luck, the stars will be out and Polaris will guide me home; my place is roughly north from here."

"What if the stars are not out?" Jenny said, in a concerned tone.

"Once I am on top of the ridge I know my way home from any direction, anyway," Jacob said, confidently. A pregnant silence followed, as Jacob pulled on his boots, over-trousers and jacket.

"I'd like to walk with you," Jenny said, surprising herself, not really wanting the relative stranger to leave her.

Jacob was also taken by surprise. "You must be mad, wanting to leave a fire like that, on a night like this! Oh, sorry: that's not the first time I've said you must be mad. No offence, I hope."

"No. But, seriously, could I come with you? I've been over the ridge in the dark many times before, but never on Christmas night. I could ring my neighbour Seb Morris to bring me back, to save you driving."

As they crossed toward the barn, light from the stable window glinted on the frost-covered, cobbled yard, like a jewelled carpet. Puddles were drum-skinned with crazed ice. They looked through the window, to see Trudy lying in a deep bed of fresh straw, with her foal lying against her. Mole was fast asleep, on top of a pile of hay bales, with his cap pulled down over his eyes, some old hessian sacks across his legs, Wellington boots still on his feet and Cloudy, the farm's sheepdog, curled up against him.

"He's never happier than when he has a newborn to guard. Calves, lambs, chickens, goslings, piglets - he pampers them all, like children. Last year, a swallows' nest fell from the beam inside the barn, so he nailed an old hat of Father's up for them. He cried when they fledged," Jenny whispered, as she gently closed the stable door.

As they left the farmyard, the bannut tree's silhouette was of a giant squid, with tentacles reaching for the heavens. A tawny owl hooted in the orchard and the night air was sweet with the scent of applewood smoke. They walked in silence for about a mile, the exertion of the climb leaving their breath drifting behind them.

They stopped where the track levelled out and the distant skyline came into view. Norton Cannon, Golden Valley, Hay

Bluff, Lord Hereford's Knob, Black Mountains and the Brecon Beacons all wallowed in the southern skyline. Above, stars circled the heavens, like jewels on an infinite velvet curtain. They stood in awe of the leaden silence and skyscape. Nothing moved, as the world slept on Christmas night.

"That's Polaris," Jacob whispered, pointing to one of a million visible stars.

"I've worked under night skies all my life, and I'm ashamed to say that I couldn't name one star. How can you be sure that's Polaris?"

"Because of the Plough. No farmer or navigator should be without a plough! Of all of the star formations, no other is more important. Look, I'll show you."

Jacob stood behind Jenny and took her right hand in his. "We'll trace out the saucepan; point your index finger."

He guided her hand along the panhandle of the Plough, naming each star: "Alkaid, Mizar, Alioth, Megrez, Phecda, then the two most important: Merak and Dubhe. Now, draw a straight line in your mind's eye, from Merak and Dubhe to the first bright star you see: and, there's Polaris, the north star. So, behind you is south, to your right is east and to left west; now, you can navigate anywhere you wish."

Jenny stared at the stars, listening to Jacob's words but not hearing them. The warmth of his hand on hers, and his overpowering presence, closed her ears and stirred her emotions. Close human contact was something she had forgotten about - something left behind, in the youth she was robbed of. She did not want this moment to end. Words died on her tongue.

"Listen to the awesome silence," Jacob whispered, still standing behind her.

She wanted to turn and face him so much, yet was afraid she was somehow dreaming. How could a stranger, who had entered her life so suddenly, in such a dramatic way and for such a brief time, have such an impact on her feelings? If she turned, the dream might end. Time stopped.

Jacob could smell her hair and wanted to touch it, but resisted. He sensed that she was crying, though her breathing was even and gave no sign of her feelings. Her arms were by her sides, like a soldier on parade. He very slowly took both of her hands in his, and gently squeezed them.

Years of disbelief and self-doubt, in her identity as a woman, ended with that small gesture. She turned to Jacob, starlight reflecting in her tears. He wiped them from her cheeks, took her hand and started toward Quarry Cottage.

They walked in total silence, on the downhill path to Earlsbrook village, each lost in their own thoughts. The church floodlights were on, bathing the shingled spire and the beech tree next to Jacob's cottage in orange light, as they walked up the path.

As Jacob unlocked the door, he broke the silence:

"Now, you have a choice to make. I can run you back home, or we can have supper by the fire and you can stay the night; the choice is yours."

Boxing Day, 2000

Jenny's mother was outside the kitchen window, wearing only her nightdress and standing barefoot in the snow. She was peering into the farm's kitchen with an angry look on her face, as the snow was falling behind her. Her father was frying bacon in Grandfather's old cast-iron pan - he was laughing. Neither spoke. Jenny was not in the room or outside; she was somewhere above, seeing everything and unable to speak, but angry with her mother.

Her eyes flashed open, from dream to reality.

Dust motes danced in a shaft of sunlight, which seared in through the cottage window, highlighting a large, willow-patterned jug and bowl, on a marble-topped washstand at the foot of the bed. Jacob was at the bedside, with two steaming mugs of coffee.

"Good morning, dreamer."

"Oh, my god! Is this real? Please tell me this is not another dream," Jenny said, clutching the duvet to her breasts.

"This is Boxing Day, in real-life, Quarry Cottage-style. And, I haven't burnt the breakfast, yet!" Jacob placed her coffee on the bedside cabinet.

Jenny stared at the blue jug, afraid to avert her gaze or speak, until she had composed herself. "What time is it?"

"Half past nine." Jacob sipped his coffee.

"The Earlsbrook Meet! I haven't missed a Boxing Day meet since I was seven; Father and I always rode with the hounds. I've been dreading this day: with Trudy in foal, I knew I couldn't ride, for the first time in years."

Jenny played for time, her mind in turmoil. This was a totally different situation to the romantic, starlit walk of last night: here was reality; end of the party; pain after pleasure... What now?

Jacob was sitting in a Lloyd Loom chair at the bedside, studying Jenny intently. "Yesterday... yesterday changed my life. I have been a fool. Money was all I knew: money, work, money... that was my life. Being with you has shown me a world of which I knew nothing. Then, there was last night! Suddenly, on the ridge, I realized that I don't want this to end - for us both to walk away, with just a brief, happy memory... Sorry, I've said too much." He stood up, with tears in his eyes, and went silently down the winding staircase to the kitchen.

Jenny's heart was a runaway train. She couldn't believe this was happening - not at her age; not so suddenly; not now!

She looked out of the bedroom window. Horse boxes were parking around the village green, and hunting people were gathering. She washed, dressed, brushed her hair and reluctantly went down the staircase. She entered the kitchen, feeling like a naughty schoolgirl.

A scrub-topped pine table was laid for two, and eggs were spitting in the pan. Jacob turned from the cooker, as she came down the stairs: "Coffee, tea or orange juice?"

She walked across the kitchen, put her arms around his neck and kissed him; "I don't want this to end, either."

*

Children on ponies, coiffured ladies on immaculately-groomed hunters, and men in hunting pink and shiny, black boots thronged the village green. The hounds were all noses and waggy tails, while whips cracked and horses steamed in the sunlight.

"Are you ready for this?" Jenny opened the cottage door.

Jacob followed her down the cottage path. They were almost at the gate, when a murmur passed through the crowd, like a ripple from a stone thrown into a mill-pond; heads turned and jaws dropped. Jenny and Jacob stood at the edge of the green, as a pregnant silence ballooned over the crowd, waiting for a pin to burst it.

Rodney Forrester, the whipper-in, stood up in his stirrups and shouted: "Riding out early this morning, Jenny?"

Laughter filled the valley, followed by a round of applause and wolf-whistles. Jenny's cheeks went from ruddy to crimson, as Jacob laughed awkwardly with them.

Phoebe Dunhill-Smith trotted toward them on her hunter. Her hunting-pink lipstick, black eyeliner and mascara were applied to perfection, and the jacket and jodhpurs she was wearing were the finest money could buy. Jenny hadn't seen her since the auction sale, and always felt defensive when she was around. This morning, Phoebe got the first shot in:

"Good morning, Jennifer. Am I to be introduced to your new friend?" She said it in a condescending manner which grated with Jacob, putting him on guard.

"Of course: this is Jacob Adams. Jacob, Phoebe Dunhill-Smith, from Court Farm."

"And, hhwhat do you do for a living, Jacob?" Phoebe said, in a haughty and condescending voice, her eyelashes fluttering like a butterfly's wings.

"Similar to you, I guess: an unemployed pest-control

operative." Jacob was back in the city, slaying giants; Jenny's eyes lit with pleasure, at his swift and incisive response.

"Oh, I see. Come along, Pegasus," Phoebe said, as she reined her horse back into the crowd.

"Wow! You soon measured her length," Jenny said, still admiring his reaction. "She's the village gossip-monger and troublemaker. She came from off, as they say. Her husband only rents the farm, but to hear her speak you'd think she owns the village. Dad could never understand how they lived such a high life: hunting, shooting and fishing, but very little farming going on."

Mole had been watching, and sidled out of the crowd toward them, pushing a rusty, old Raleigh bike, which Jacob guessed must be at least fifty years old.

"I wondered where yer was, missus. I bin knockin' the back door an' 'ollerin' at the bedroom winder at 'ome; I wanted yer ter see the lickle 'orse: 'e's sucklin'."

*

The foal was standing on shaky legs, by his mother's side. Trudy whinnied a greeting, as soon as she saw Jenny opening the stable door. Jacob watched, enthralled at the demonstration of love and understanding which existed between human and horse. The proud mother allowed Jenny to run her hands all over the newborn, stroking and comforting both as she did so.

"All's well," Jenny said; "seems a fine young fellow."

She walked back toward Jacob, just as Mole came pedalling into the yard on his bike.

"What yer think of 'im, missus? 'E's a good un, in't 'e!

What yer ganna call 'im?"

She looked at Jacob, then back at Mole. "Jake... Midnight Jake, after my new friend." Jenny smiled at Jacob, with the seed of a tear in her eye, which hinted at sadness laced with joy.

"I 'ope the lickle 'orse in't as frit o' geese as 'e' is!" Mole said, chuckling toward Jacob with a toothless giggle.

Jenny and Jacob returned to the house, leaving Mole with the horses.

Jenny was making coffee, when Jacob said the words she had been dreading: "I'm afraid I have to leave for London soon, to finalize accounts; I'm putting the flat on the market and tying up loose ends. I hate having to leave, after such an unexpectedly perfect two days, but I'm meeting the estate agent at ten in the morning."

Jenny felt her heart sink. Swept along by events, she had given little thought to where they went from here. She had known that they would have to part sooner or later - alas, this was the sooner.

"Home-made chicken and mushroom soup with fresh bread, before you go?" Jenny asked, looking away and trying to sound nonchalant.

"That would be great, thank you." Jacob paused, then continued: "I still can't believe this is happening."

"It's only a bowl of chicken soup!" she said, trying to lighten the moment.

Jenny turned to see him sitting in her father's place at the table. "Mother has allowed no one to sit in that place, in that chair, ever since Father died - it's lovely to see it being used again. I feel as though the pall of gloom which has hung over this house ever since has at last been lifted."

As they sat, quietly absorbing the poignancy of the

moment, a tortoiseshell butterfly, prematurely woken from hibernation by the warmth of the kitchen, flew between them and settled in the folds of the curtain.

"That... is one very significant butterfly!" Jacob said.

New Year's Day, 2001

Jenny awoke to a wood pigeon, cooing from the guttering above her bedroom window, and an unusually mild southerly breeze, purring through the bannut-tree branches. The net curtains billowed high, like indoor cumulus clouds, as she roused from fitful sleep.

She had spoken to Jacob many times by phone, when he was in London. Each time she came off the line, she was left wondering if it was all a crazy dream, which could easily turn into a living nightmare. One question burned in her mind, above all others: was she being naively foolish, to think that real love happened to a woman her age?

She showered, dressed and went downstairs, her mind still musing as she put the kettle on the stove to boil. Cloudy was scratching at the back door for his ritual morning milk.

Her thoughts came to an abrupt halt, as a white van drove into the farmyard. A young, blonde-haired woman with a ponytail got out, carrying a long, flat, cardboard box. Jenny went outside to investigate.

"Mrs. Montfort?" the girl said, as she approached.

"*Miss* Montfort," Jenny said, correcting her.

"Who's a lucky girl, then?" the girl giggled, her blonde hair blowing wildly in the breeze.

"That depends what it is!"

"Signature, please," the girl said, holding out an order pad.

"What am I signing for, first?" Jenny was agitated by the

flouncy attitude of the girl, yet intrigued by the box.

"Well, I'm from Telepetal, so it could be flowers!" the girl said, in a condescending tone.

Jenny's heart pounded, as she heard the word *flowers*. She signed the pad and whispered "thank you" to the girl.

"Enjoy!" the blonde said, bouncing back to her van.

Jenny carried the box into the kitchen, placing it in her father's place at the table, and pictured Jacob in his chair. Never having had a bouquet before, she was almost afraid to open it. Checking the label several times, in case there had been a mistake, she eased the ribbon from the corner and lifted the lid. Eighteen deep-red roses lay in a bed of cream tissue. Jenny stared at them in disbelief, her fingers trembling, as she lifted the accompanying envelope.

"Thank you for making my Christmas the most complete ever, and here's wishing us a Happy New Year!
Jacob.
XXX"

Her mind went back to his departure and the "significant butterfly" moment. She looked up at the curtain and, as she did so, the tortoiseshell opened and closed its wings, just once.

"Thank you, butterfly; I'll take that as semaphore for good luck," she whispered, and kissed the note.

Jenny cut several hazel twigs, laden with catkins, from the orchard hedgerow - yellow pollen drifted from them, as she walked back to the house. She took the old, enamel jug from the dairy, in which her father used to carry the household milk. Caressing the handle, his words rang in her ears, as he came through the door: "Loverly, loverly milk, straight from cow to cornflakes!"

She arranged the roses and catkins, recalling the countless times she had picked wild flowers whilst dreaming of a real bouquet from a real lover. Now, she had both, but the doubts still nagged.

Glancing out of the window, she realized that the farmyard was full of smoke.

"Oh, my god, no; not the barn!" She ran across the yard to find Mole behind the cider house, making a bonfire of old sacks and boxes.

"What the bloody hell are you doing, Mole? I thought the barn was on fire!"

"'Avin' a clear-out... Whatja think?"

Jenny stood with hands firmly on hips, looking nonplussed. "But, you haven't had a clear-out in the barn for the last four decades! Why now? Why today?"

"'Cause it's New Year's Day... and 'cause we've never 'ad a new boss, in the last four whatyercall'ums. But I'd say, by the way yer've bin behavin' and the look on yer face when 'e arrives, that we're just about ter get one. So, I'm clearin' out the barn. Any more bloody stupid questuns?"

January 2nd, 2001

"**N**ice arrangement!" Jacob said, walking in through the open door and taking Jenny by surprise.

She looked at him in disbelief that he had returned - that he was real.

"I loved the flowers! Thank you! Two days... Two days - that's all we had together - and I missed you so much!"

"I've missed you, too! I couldn't wait to get back to Earlsbrook. How can it be that we've only known one another for a few days, and we feel like this?" Jacob said, surprising her that he felt the same way, too.

"Perhaps we should walk on the ridge. My mind has been in a whirl, ever since the auction sale; walking always seems to blow the cobwebs away."

"Sounds good to me. Let's go." Jacob walked toward the door.

*

Jenny coaxed her battered 4x4 up the drover's road, to Midnight Ridge. Ragged pieces of canopy, from Jacob's dramatic rooftop entrance, swung about wildly, as they climbed the hill.

Snowdrops on the banks pushed into sunlight, and lengthening days gave the hills a sense of optimism. On the ridge, high cirrus clouds reached across from the Welsh border, like a witch's fingers. To the south, between the Malvern Hills and Skirrid, a blue haze merged land seamlessly into sky. The season was winter, but the heart of spring was beating.

Jacob got out of the truck, taking Jenny's hand in his. In all of her years as a single woman, she had ached for close contact with someone other than family. But, now it was happening to her, and she was free to enjoy the moment, her inner voice kept saying that it was all too good to last.

"Will you walk to Martha's Tump with me?" Jenny said, opening the truck's door. "I'm sorry, I just need to clear my mind."

As they started on the long, ridgetop path, the sound of human voices drove a wing of golden plover to flight, from within the dead bracken. Rising above the horizon, their light underwings flashed in unison, as they turned against the greyness of the clouds, landing again, almost as soon as they had taken off. The path sloped gently downward, toward Martha's Tump. Jacob hadn't been to this part of the ridge since he was a boy.

Jenny walked ahead of him, until they came to her "Queen of the Castle" rock. The sadness of her last visit seemed a lifetime away. "This is my rock," Jenny said, as she sat astride it, patting it like a horse's rump.

Jacob walked a few paces in front, waiting for her to open the conversation. He stood in silence, looking down the escarpment, which scrambled down to the village. Silence was a powerful tool, which Jacob always used in business, to close deals; today, he waited for Jenny to open. The church clock sprinkled its midday chimes onto the breeze, as Jacob turned his back on the sun to face her.

Jenny knew she was in love and she ached to tell him. Yet,

she also felt that if she allowed her love to fly free and he let her down, she would never be able to love again. This was her first and last chance at happiness, so it had to be right.

"The last time I sat on this rock, in October, I was in pieces: Mother had just died, and I looked down at her grave knowing that life, as I had known it, was at an end. My father and I were very close, but Mother and I were not. Every time I had a boyfriend, she killed the relationship dead, and I hated her for it. Before Father died, I promised I would look after her. And, I fulfilled that promise: for four years I kept the farm going and cared for Mother.

"After she died, I decided I would sell the stock and take time to consider my future. After sale day, all I had was Mole, Cloudy, Eric the goose, a few chickens and a pregnant mare, all of whom were dependent on me.

"Then, I go for a drive on Christmas Eve, to clear my head, and a man falls through the roof of my truck! On Christmas night I slept with him; on Boxing Day he left me; and on New Year's Day he returned! To tell you the truth, I'm... very happy... but, scared it's all too good to be true... for both of us."

Jacob was still facing her, saying nothing. All air movement had ceased around them, as Jenny's eyes burnt into Jacob's, searching for an answer. He walked slowly toward her, looking deep into her eyes.

"Work was my god. Money, deals, risk, and pressure were sustenance, sport and pleasure. Then, for no apparent reason, I stopped enjoying it, wanting something else from life, yet not knowing what. Three days before Christmas, I decided to quit. I don't take decisions without thinking through the consequences, so I came to Quarry Cottage to find space and time to regroup. Then, I went for a bike ride, fell through a roof and... fell in love! I cannot explain why; I am not normally impulsive. I had the best Christmas of my life, saw a foal born and have never felt as happy as I did that day.

"When I left for London, the parting gave me plenty of time to reflect. Yet, all the time I was away, I had the urge to return, as soon as I could: I missed you, the farm, the horses, the tranquillity and peace of the countryside, and - dare I say it – Mole; I couldn't wait to come back here. Now I have, nothing has changed. I don't know what your feelings are, or where we go from here; all I know is... I love you!"

A red kite flew overhead, its white underwings thrusting hard into the breeze.

Jenny was sitting silently on her rock, the tear tracks down her cheeks glistening in the sun. "I never imagined, in my wildest dreams, that the next time I sat here I would be crying tears of joy. You've answered my question. Thank you."

She stood up and walked toward Jacob. "I didn't realize love could be so sudden; so all consuming; so unexpected. I thought it would be a gradual thing, like spring coming." She kissed him. He hugged her.

March, 2001

Jenny lay awake on the hotel bed, in a room overlooking Cardigan Bay. Gulls drifted past the window on rigid wings, gliding silently through morning sunlight, while orange wave crests broke in an arc across the river estuary; the low purr of breaking waves mixed with the rhythmic sound of Jacob's breathing, as he slept beside her. She had never stayed in a hotel before, never woke looking out to sea, and never lain awake so happy and content. Sliding silently out of bed, to sit in the bay window, she gazed at a world that she knew existed, but had never experienced. Tears of love filled her eyes, as she looked back at Jacob, sleeping.

After several minutes his eyes opened, sensing through semi-consciousness that she was no longer beside him. He looked at her silhouette against the morning light, for long, silent seconds, before speaking.

"Happy or sad?" he said, knowing that her tears could mean either. She did not immediately answer.

A gannet towered into the air, then dived into breaking waves, before bobbing up like a cork, to swallow the fish it had speared.

"Elated; wondrous; awestruck! I don't know what else to say. I've gazed at the horizon from Midnight Ridge, watched the sun rise, the storm clouds billow and the forest on Sheepcratch Hill burn crimson in the setting sun; I've watched silver arrows laying vapour trails across the sky, on the way to

America. And now, here I am on the edge of Wales, part of the horizon, and I can't believe it's real." Jenny paused, looking back out to sea, and added: "You've travelled and I haven't."

"Maybe, but I'd never seen a foal born, been chased by a goose, had a bonfire or lived by the seasons. There are no seasons in the city, only cold days and hot, unbearable sticky-shirt days; days when I longed to be on my bike, instead of writing a presentation, or dealing with human vermin."

After breakfast, they walked on the Pembrokeshire coast path to Jacob's favourite vantage point, to watch guillemots, fulmar and razorbills, battling for ownership of perilous ledges, over boiling waters. Jenny sat on a grassy bank, among tufts of thrift and heather, as Jacob stood beside her. They watched the spectacular wildlife in silence. After dinner they walked to a clifftop bench below the hotel, to watch the sunset. Canada geese skimmed wave crests, honking as they flew to roost, and the sea quenched the ochre sun.

Jacob broke the silence: "We could get married, here on this clifftop."

Jenny stared, open-mouthed, at Jacob, considering her answer. At length, she said: "We could... all three of us!"

"You, me and Mole, I suppose?" Jacob joked.

"No... You, me and the baby."

"WHAT?" Jacob shouted, scaring some oystercatchers from a rock. "You mean you're... you're..."

"Pregnant is the word you're looking for."

"Jacob Adams, a bloody father? I don't believe it!" An ear-to-ear grin spread across his face.

"Well, I can assure you it isn't Mole's!"

"How... How do you know? Are you sure?"

"Well, I thought I'd started the change, but the doctor

confirmed it, before we came away. I didn't know what to say, or how you would react. Then, you mentioned marriage, so I thought: it's now or never!"

*

Mole sat in his chair and took a cold bacon sandwich from his battered tin. The farmyard was silent. March used to be the busiest month of the year: all lambs, ewes, afterbirth and bottles of milk; today, the only noise was the rookery behind the barn: a swirling, cackling cacophony of sound, with the nesting season in full motion. Mole had never been in sole charge of Poplar Farm before, and was continuing his barn clearance while he had the chance. He had unearthed the cider press and scratter, from beneath decades of farm debris: baler twine; paper bags; broken forks; mole traps; rat traps; cobwebs; dust; rat and mouse droppings...

Then, he remembered the box. Only he and the boss knew where it was hidden, and now the boss was dead.

He threw the crust from his bacon sandwich to Cloudy, who swallowed it in one gulp. Scraping hay debris from the floor, behind the cider mill, he decided to check the contents while no one else was around the farm to disturb him. The thick, oak board above the box was stuck fast, with several years of encrusted dirt around the edge, forming a tight seal with its neighbours. Scraping around it with his pocket-knife, he eased it open.

Heaving the old ammunition box out of the hole took more effort than he remembered. He placed it on the bench underneath the window, opened it and untied a boot-lace securing the neck of a leather bag, inside. He thrust his hand into the bag.

"Well, boss, it's still all here, by the look of it!" he said to himself, whilst holding a gleaming handful of coins to the sunlight.

As he did so, Cloudy barked a warning at the barn door, as though someone was coming. He put the coins back in the bag, closed the lid, dropped it into the hole and kicked hay back over it, as Eddie the postman walked across the yard, pushed a letter into the letterbox and left.

"Yer silly bugger! Yer frit me! It's only Eddie - yer knows 'im!" Cloudy crawled back underneath the chair, his tail between his legs.

Mole went out to the orchard, to check on Trudy and Midnight Jake. The foal was running around on sturdy legs beneath the apple trees, as Trudy looked up at Mole and whinnied a greeting of contentment. Mole leant on the gate.

"Well, boss; I 'ope you're lookin' down on this. The cattle a' gone, no bloody lambs or ewes left, no tups ter feed, but I'm still lookin' after the 'orse. That's a fine foal exermasizin' his legs round the orchard. Ooh, an' there's blossom buds on the russet tree."

He removed his cap to scratch his pure white, bald pate, adding: "The missus'll soon be back; dunna fret - 'er's up in Wales, 'avin' the rust rubbed off 'er."

*

"It feels as though we've been away for three weeks, not three days," Jenny said, as Jacob turned onto the farm's driveway. "Well, the barn's still in one piece. Oh, my god! Look at Midnight Jake, trotting around the orchard!"

As they got out of the car, Mole shouted across the yard: "'Ave yer seen the lickle 'orse a gallopin'?"

"Home, sweet bloody home! Mole shouting from the barn doorway, goose-shit on the doorstep and my mother's clothes still on top of the plate-rack. And, now you're leaving me again, for London," Jenny said, opening the kitchen door.

"I only have to tie up a few loose ends; a couple of days at most. I'm seeing the solicitor and finalizing things at the bank, now that the flat's sold – then, I'll be at Quarry Cottage full time. I can't wait. Then, we can make plans for the three of us!"

Jenny watched Jacob's car leave the yard, and went over to the orchard gate, to look at Midnight Jake. As she came back by the barn, Mole shouted to her:

"I've got somethin' to show yer, missus; come in 'ere."

The barn was always her father's domain - now it was Mole's. A man's world of farm clutter. Similarly, the old dairy was hers: egg boxes, fruit crates, scales and medicines for the animals.

Mole seemed agitated, quiet and fidgety. "Yer dad told me I was not ter show any bugger, but that was when 'e was alive, o' course. Now 'e's bloody gone, and I'm the only one as knows."

"Knows what?"

"I'll show yer." He went behind the cider mill, scraped hay off of the floor with his boot, lifted the board and pulled out the ammunition box. He passed the small, leather bag to Jenny: "'Ere y'are. Open it."

Jenny took the heavy bag, undid the bow and looked inside. "Oh, my god! Gold coins!"

"Sovereigns and 'alf sovereigns - dozens o' the buggers!"

Mole said, as he pulled another bag from the box.

"Whose are they? How did they get there?"

"They wuz mine. If anythin' 'appened ter me, they wuz gunna be the boss's. Rainy day money, see? Now the boss inna 'ere, an' now they'm gunna be yer babby's."

"What do you mean, 'gonna be my babby's'?"

"Well, yer pregnant, in't yer?"

"How do you know that?"

"I knowed yer was pregnant afore you did! Colour of yer eyes, roses in yer cheeks - same as an 'orse, see: shiny coat; glint in th'eye... I always know when they bin covered, an' I knew you 'ad."

"I can't believe you've just said that, Mole! You never bloody-well cease to amaze me! Where the hell have all these coins come from?"

"Victorian, most of 'em. They wuz me grandad's, then me dad's, then mine. Now the boss is gone an', like I said, they'm fer yer babby now; I shanna want 'em."

"Are you saying my father knew these were here, for all those years, and never said anything to anyone?"

"Far as I know. Somebody 'ad ter be told now, in case I snuffed it! Now yer know."

*

March winds were blowing spring into the hills of the Welsh Marches. Skeletal hawthorns were showing emerald-green, as cowslips pushed skyward, nodding like happy schoolchildren. A blackbird was busy gathering mud, to line its nest.

Jacob's car bounced and splashed its way through the puddled track leading to Poplar Farm, as Jenny was in the orchard, setting traps between the dozens of molehills which had appeared during winter.

Jacob felt as though he had springs in his feet, as he approached the orchard gateway.

"My poor orchard; it looks more like a relief map of the Pyrenees. Bloody moles!" Jenny said, as she walked toward Jacob. "Welcome back to the real world."

"No moles in London; only the rat race. But, I'm back, thank God! Finances settled; bank happy; solicitor sorted and paid up; office door closed, for the last time - no more wheeler-dealing with devious bastards!" Jacob said, as he hugged Jenny.

She opened the kitchen door. "Look," she said, pointing to the kitchen stove: "at last, Mother's clothes have gone to the charity shop and the house has had a spring clean - the first one for years. Mole has finished his barn clearance and, as ever, completely amazed me with his observations."

"Like what?"

"He told me I was pregnant, before I had chance to tell him."

"How the hell did he know that?"

"By comparing me to a bloody pregnant mare: shiny coat and a glint in my eye!"

"Neigh!"

"Oh, very funny! Any more comments like that and you can buzz off back to your rats in London!"

Jenny poured coffee and they sat at the kitchen table.

"Not only did he tell me I was pregnant, he proceeded to pull a box of gold sovereigns from a hole in the barn floor - I was flabbergasted. Do you know what he said?"

Jacob shrugged his shoulders: "I have no idea."

"They're fer yer babby, now yer dad's dead. According to Mole, my dad knew they were there, but he never said a word to me."

"Whose were they?"

"Mole's, handed down through his family. He's last in line and wanted my dad to have them, if he popped his clogs, but Dad went first. Then, he somehow deduced that I was pregnant and decided that my baby should inherit them. It's a bit like having a mind-reader living in the barn: he knows what I'm doing before I do."

"Where are the coins now?"

"Back in the cider-house floor, I expect."

Jacob finished his coffee and stood to leave.

"I had my bike repaired, when I was in the Smoke. I think I'll go back to the cottage, unload the car and take the bike over Midnight Ridge, to try it out. Will you come to me for supper? I've brought some edible goodies to celebrate my retirement. Say, seven o'clock? That'll give me time for a shower after my ride, and to prepare the meal."

*

Phoebe Dunhill-Smith rode out from Court Farm stables, on her favourite hunter, toward Earlsbrook village. She derived great pleasure from seeing curtains move and heads turn, assuming that the locals were admiring her, trotting by on Pegasus. The afternoon was hers to enjoy: husband Henry had taken a party of local farmers pigeon shooting, on newly-planted corn, below Midnight Ridge.

The horse knew every twist, turn and pothole in the track, leading to the ridge; there was little for Phoebe to do, other than enjoy the ride. She had no knowledge of the accident which had led to Jenny and Jacob's meeting, and was now about to ride over the very spot where it had happened.

As she did, Pegasus baulked, whinnied and did a curious side-step, as though nervous, or sensing that something had happened there.

"Whoa, darling! What's the matter?" Phoebe said, as she patted the side of his neck, to calm him. After a few yards, he steadied, and they continued the slow ascent to the ridge.

They rode up onto her favourite little knoll, high above Court Farm, and she dismounted to admire her husband's rolling acres, as Pegasus stood beside her, nibbling at the sparse grass. A solitary raven flew past at eye level, followed by a flock of wood pigeons, dropping down toward the farm.

As they flew over a hawthorn hedge, a barrage of gunshots from Henry and his friends shattered the silence.

Pegasus reared, snatching the loosely-held reins from Phoebe's hand. He bolted between two gorse bushes and disappeared, toward the crest of the ridge.

*

Jacob arrived at the east end of the ridge. The steady climb to the top had been muddy, and despite the new tyres he'd had fitted, he could feel the wheels spinning on the gradient, as he powered down on the bike's pedals. It was an exhausting ascent. He realized how out of condition he was after being in London, but it was just what he needed. He stopped to get his breath back and soak up the atmosphere.

The skylarks had arrived on the ridge for nesting, their trilling notes like airborne music, tumbling from the fluffy cumulus clouds which lolled over the hills. He stood listening to them and felt the burden of work lifting from his shoulders; at last, he had time and space in his life to fill the lonely void he had carried in his head for so many years.

Meeting Jenny had come at exactly the right time. The only deal with her was contentment, happiness and prospective fatherhood.

He had always thought that parenting was something other people did, not him. Until now, that was. He imagined holding his own baby and, as it grew, teaching it about the birds, the stars, and sharing its life. The future looked good.

He remounted his bike and took the long, undulating, grass track westward. He could see the pine trees where he had first met Jenny in the distance, and pedalled toward them. He was enjoying the easy-going ride when he noticed the twenty or so moorland ponies which frequented the centre-ground of the ridge, running through the heather and bracken – it was something he had not seen before. Their heads and flowing manes were only just visible above the gorse; they were some distance away, heading south. They appeared to be in full flight from something. He stopped to watch the spectacle, enjoying the sense of freedom that they enshrined.

Then, he noticed that the lead horse was much taller and powerful looking than the main group. It was carrying an empty saddle, with stirrups flailing wildly, from side to side. The ponies were following, but losing ground.

"Jesus, someone's been thrown!" he said aloud, to himself. He could not see where the rider was.

The big horse was going round in an arc - Jacob guessed it was following the public footpath, which wound its way across the ridge. He decided to continue in that direction, in case the fallen rider needed help. Remounting, he followed the path between the gorse, toward the pine trees.

Then, some way ahead, he saw a figure running through the heather, arms waving and shouting. Jacob had his head down, and was pedalling hard, just as Pegasus cleared the track-side gorse bush.

As Pegasus appeared, his lead hoof hit Jacob's temple, shattering his helmet. Phoebe saw him fall.

"Oh, my god, no!" she screamed, as her horse disappeared out of sight.

*

Jenny was crossing the farmyard, to try a halter on Midnight Jake, for the first time, and Mole was standing by the stable door, waiting for her, as the air-ambulance flew high above the farm, toward the ridge. Mole watched it drop down toward the pine trees.

"Some bugger's in trouble," he said, opening the stable door.

"Jacob's gone up there on his bike," Jenny said, looking concerned; "I hope it's not him."

"Bloody fools a shootin', I 'spect - I 'eard 'em bangin', afore."

Jenny managed to get the halter onto Midnight Jake, after some head-shaking and nudging from Trudy. Then, she walked him around the stable a couple of times, and out into the orchard. Considering it was his first time out, mother and foal walked side-by-side very well. She walked them several times around the orchard, before taking them back to the stable and bedding them down.

As she came out of the door, Seb Morris, from Village Farm, drove into the yard on his tractor, at speed. He got out of the cab and walked toward her.

"Hello, Seb. You're looking a bit glum," Jenny said, as he approached.

"Yer'd better go inside," he gestured toward the house.

"Why? What's the matter?"

"Come inside. It enna good news I'a come with!"

"NO! NO! Not the air-ambulance!? Not Jacob!?"

"I'm sorry, girl: they a took 'im away; 'e never stood a chance! The bloody 'orse come over a gorse bush at 'im... an' that was it. I was up there lookin' at the sheep; I seen it all."

"Horse? What bloody horse? What do you mean?"

"That there fancy Phoebe, from Court Farm: 'er 'orse just bolted when 'e 'eard the guns; 'it 'im duff! Lucky she 'ad 'er phone with 'er. Some walkers on the path tried ter save 'im, but it was no good."

Jenny stood in stunned silence, her legs buckling as she took in the words. Then, Mole ran across the yard and grabbed her arm, as she sank to her knees in the mud.

May, 2001

It had been eight weeks since the accident, and grief filled every waking second of Jenny's days. Her nights were spent in fitful spasms, staring into darkness and making endless cups of tea, or crying. Concentration was impossible, even on the simplest of tasks.

But, carrying Jacob's baby was the most joyous thing that had ever happened to her. To be sharing a new life with him and his child would have meant the fulfilment of her wildest dream, after all the void years of her life.

That Jacob's death had been a tragic accident was an inescapable fact. But, that it was the Dunhill-Smiths who had caused it was acid, burning into Jenny's heart. And, that neither of them had offered a word of regret or condolence since gnawed at her sanity.

Staring into a void of misery, she decided that she must do something about that, before it consumed her and her unborn child.

She climbed into her truck and drove to Court Farm. Pegasus watched from his stable, as she drove into the yard. Henry saw her arrive and rushed into the house, to warn Phoebe. Jenny hesitated, glaring at the horse which had taken Jacob away from her, before opening her vehicle's door. "You must do it," she whispered to herself.

As she walked across the yard, she could see Phoebe standing at the back of the kitchen, watching her. She knocked on the door and Henry opened it.

They stared at one another, but neither spoke, both waiting for a reaction from the other.

"Yes?" Henry said, at length.

Jenny's eyes burned into his, waiting for some sign that she was to be allowed in or, at least, that Phoebe would come to the door and speak to her. Neither happened.

"Is that all you have to say?" Jenny said, as her eyes filled with tears.

"We have been instructed by our lawyers in London that we should have no contact with you. Please leave our yard."

Jenny turned and walked back to her vehicle. Hatred dried her tears.

June, 2001

J enny watched the post-van leave the yard - a rare event, since her farm was no longer active; post now was occasional, rather than daily.

A large, official-looking envelope lay on the kitchen floor, which was even more unusual. Around a small, blue logo, the writing read: *"Small, Bent and Madement, Solicitors."* It was addressed to her, but she had never heard of them. She took her father's paper-knife from the shelf.

> *Dear Miss Montfort,*
> **Re: Jacob Elijah Adams, deceased**
>
> *Please accept our condolences for the sudden and sad loss of Jacob. We have been his legal advisers throughout his career and knew him well. His death came as a great shock to us all.*
>
> *As you are no doubt aware, he had just taken steps to retire, take his pension and close down his business. As a result of this, he recently visited us, and his financial advisers, to wind up his pension scheme, consolidate his investments for income and leave his legal affairs in order.*
>
> *Jacob had no close living relatives, from either side of his family, had never married*

and had no children.   It may come as a shock to you that you were left as the main beneficiary.   There were some minor gifts in his will, but the bulk goes to you.   We also know that he had, at last, found personal happiness with you; he contacted us recently, advising us of your pregnancy.   A codicil was added to his existing will, to provide for your child, should you pre-decease him.

Probate has been applied for, and we attach a list of assets which will be transferred to your name, once probate has been received. This list, as you will see, includes the contents of and freehold to Quarry Cottage, Earlsbrook.   The estimated gross value of the estate comes to £2,766,590.00, after deduction of inheritance tax due.   We will be pleased to continue acting as your legal advisers, should you wish to use our services.

We will be in touch once probate has been received.

Once again, please accept our sympathy at this sad time.

Yours sincerely,
Sandra J. Small (Senior Partner).

September, 2001

Jenny sat in her truck at the spot where Jacob died, stone-faced, as she had every day since the accident, asking why. No answer ever came. So, she drove back down to the farm, parked and walked over to the cider house.

Her back was aching. With her baby due in two weeks, she was relying on Mole to carry her workload. Walking was laborious. Mole was very helpful - at times, overly so, to the point of annoying her, and she couldn't help snapping at him, which she always regretted. She could now see him in the paddock, through the barn's open door.

"Mole, why the hell haven't you put the horses in the stable yet?" she shouted.

As she turned from the doorway, a sudden, jabbing pain made her grab the doorframe, for support. She managed to sit down on a bale of hay, as a strong contraction overwhelmed her.

"Mole!" she screamed. "For Christ's sake, come!"

As he appeared in the doorway, her waters broke.

"Bloody 'ell, missus! Are yer 'avin the babby?"

"Well, I hope it's not a bloody lamb!" she groaned, through the pain.

"If it was, I'd know what ter do!"

"Get on your bike and fetch Mrs. Morris... NOW!"

*

Seb Morris bounced up the drive to Poplar Farm on his tractor, with Mrs. Morris hanging on the back like a Roman charioteer. Mole was pedalling like fury behind them.

"'Er's in the cider 'ouse, missus. I'll fetch somethin' fer 'er ter 'ave the babby on," Mole said, panting for breath and pointing at the door.

Mrs. Morris entered, to find Jenny between contractions and the baby's head partly visible. She was about to shout to Seb, when Mole appeared in the doorway, carrying a bale of barley straw.

"Towels! Sheets! Anything - but not bloody straw!" Mrs. Morris shouted at Mole. "She's not calving!"

*

The baby boy suckled, contentedly. Jenny gazed at him, in loving awe of the new life she and Jacob had created.

"Jacob Montfort-Adams, you are as beautiful as your father." Her voice cracked with emotion, as tears of joy streamed down her cheeks.

The midwife opened the bedroom door and smiled. "Oh, Jenny, what can I say? It seems I'm a little bit late, to say the least! I'm so sorry. But, I'm told by Mrs. Morris that you had expert attention, and didn't need me, anyway... you even had clean straw! That's better than you would have had in a hospital!"

"Poor Mole; poor Mrs. Morris - they've both been wonderful. If only my baby had four legs, everything would have been perfect!" Jenny bit her lip, to hide the mixture of joy and sadness she felt.

There was a knock at the bedroom door, and Mole's face

appeared. "Can I come in an' see the babby, missus?" He scratched his bald head and blushed, leaving a trail of hayseeds across the bedroom carpet.

"'E's a fine lickle babby! The boss 'ad a liked ter seen 'im sucklin'. Strong as a foal!"

"Mole, how can I thank you?"

"'E'll be able ter ride the lickle 'orse in no time. I'll get 'im a lickle saddle."

September, 2014
Earlsbrook Village Show

The ringside loudspeaker crackled into life:

"The next competitor in today's junior event is thirteen-year-old Jacob Montfort-Adams, riding Midnight Jake. Most of you saw them riding to fourth position at last year's show. Since then, they've had one win and a second to their credit; they seem to improve each time out. So, no pressure, Jacob!"

"Come on, Midnight, let's show them," Jacob said, cantering up to the first fence and clearing it. He took the next seven without fault, with only the water jump left for a clear round. Midnight Jake shook his head and jumped, clearing the water by a yard. Applause came as his hooves hit the ground.

"Clear round - the first of the day! Well done, Jacob!"

Jenny stood by the horsebox, waiting for him, feeling pride and sadness in one jumbled emotion. "If only your father could see us now," she whispered.

The loudspeaker crackled again:

"Our next rider also comes from the village - this is her debut event. Please welcome Ella Dunhill-Smith, riding Equuleus, which I am reliably informed means 'Little Horse'. Away you go, Ella!"

Phoebe Dunhill-Smith stood up from her ringside seat, clapping her hands high in the air. "That's my girl," she said, in a loud voice, looking around to ensure that everyone had heard her.

Ella took the first three fences well, fell off at the fourth, remounted and finished the round with twelve faults. Phoebe stood and walked away, in silence.

The years had done little to alter the pain Jenny felt upon hearing the name Dunhill-Smith. She had been compensated by their insurers, and was very well provided for from Jacob's estate, but the money was of little comfort or consolation for the loss. Jenny felt no animosity toward little Ella, but could not resist a little schadenfreude taking control of her emotions, as Phoebe walked away from ringside with her head down. In the fourteen years since Jacob had died, she had still not made any contact with Jenny, nor shown any remorse.

*

"What's for tea, Mum?" Jacob asked, rubbing his belly as he put his trophy on the kitchen shelf.

"You're forever hungry! Go and feed the horses, then your tea will be on the table when you come in."

Jacob took a slice of cake from the cupboard and went outside to the stable. As he crossed the yard, he noticed the cider house door ajar, and went over to shut it.

The light was on. "Are you in there, Mole?" Jacob shouted.

No reply came, so he switched the light off and went toward the stable.

Mole was lying face down and motionless in the yard, clutching a bundle of hay under his arm. Jacob ran for the house.

September, 2014
Mole's funeral

Seb Morris trundled up the drive to Poplar Farm, on his tractor; the steel rims of the Victorian dray he was towing rattled and clattered over stones, and through potholes. He parked in front of Mole's beloved cider house.

Jack "The Measurer" Black arrived, in his grey undertaker's van, and got out to unload the bier and coffin - Eric the goose eyed him, as he opened the rear doors. Jack had his head and arms in the van, as Eric ran across the yard, aiming for his rear with wings outstretched, neck poker-straight and beak agape.

Seb Morris intercepted him, sinking a polished funeral shoe into his plumage. "Bugger off, you crazy goose! Yer nearly lost yer weddin' tackle then, Jack! Lucky I was 'ere on time." Eric took the hint and walked away.

They wheeled the coffin across the yard and slid it onto the dray. "D'yer think many'll come?" Seb said, as they positioned the coffin.

"'Ard ter say. 'E wus a popular old sod. Knowin' the locals, they'll all turn up, 'opin' ter find out where 'e's 'idden 'is money. Never spent a bloody penny an' worked the land all them years! A lot'll come just fer the bun fight at the village 'all, after," Jack said, tightening a lorry strap across the coffin.

"Some say 'e's got land, but I never found out where it wus. Me dad said 'e used ter pinch swedes from our fields, when 'e wus young: too tight ter buy 'em. An' 'e said yer never saw 'im without a rabbit 'angin' from 'is belt."

Seb walked toward the cider house, emerging with Mole's cap, which he placed atop the coffin. Cloudy stood in the doorway, his tail between his legs, looking forlorn.

Jenny came out of the kitchen door, followed by Jacob, walking awkwardly behind her, not knowing quite how to act at his first funeral. She placed a bunch of home-grown dahlias on the coffin, tied with a plait of barley straw, then she walked over to the cider house and stroked Cloudy's head. He looked up at her with sad eyes and pawed her, leaving a muddy mark down the front of her black funeral skirt.

"Thanks, Cloudy. That one's for Mole, I suppose! Mud, hayseeds, grease and rust were his trademarks; he'll be happy with that."

"'Orse muck would a' bin more apt," Seb added.

"We'd better get going: the vicar's got three ter put underground today," Jack Black said, checking the coffin for stability. He added: "That's the first time I've ever seen 'im on four wheels; only ever seen 'im on two, or in his Wellies!"

As Seb started the tractor, Cloudy ran across the yard, jumped on the dray and sat on top of the coffin, next to Mole's cap.

"Well, I'll be buggered! Just look at that," Jack said.

The dray rumbled down the drive, with Cloudy balancing on all fours, on top of the coffin. Jenny and Jacob followed in the truck.

Dozens of villagers stood around the lychgate, while in the lane six bearers awaited instructions from Jack Black. The graveyard was packed with mourners.

Cloudy lay stubbornly on the coffin's lid, refusing to

move and growling at anyone who approached. When Jack Black walked forward to take control, reaching to pull Cloudy off, the dog snarled a warning. When Jack went to grab his collar, Cloudy bit him, drawing blood.

Jacob saw what had happened and offered Cloudy the back of his hand. The dog licked it, raising his paw in return, but still would not move.

Reverend Elwyn Elkins was anxious to get going, and started toward the doorway:

"I am the resurrection and the life, sayeth the Lord. He that believeth in me, though he were dead, yet shall he live, and whosoever liveth and believeth in me shall never die."

So, Mole entered the church on the bearers' shoulders, with Cloudy sitting proudly on top of the coffin, as Jacob walked behind, holding his paw. All pews were taken, the choir stalls full and the walls lined with mourners. As the cortege came down the aisle, the congregation turned as one to see the spectacle; a trickle of giggles became a tsunami of laughter, as Mole and Cloudy came to rest in front of the altar.

Cloudy started whining and yapping at Jacob.

"Quiet, boy," Jacob whispered. "Come on down." The dog stood, took Mole's cap in his teeth, then jumped from the coffin, leaning against Jacob's legs.

Reverend Elkins tried to contain himself and retain some solemnity, before starting the service. Finally, the laughter subsided and he continued:

"We are here today to celebrate the life of our brother Samuel Gillion, affectionately known to us all as Mole. Birthright may bring wealth or poverty, but death makes all men equal. We are here today, as Samuel becomes equal to all that have passed this way before him."

Prayers were said, then the congregation sang "Plough the Fields and Scatter". Afterward, Reverend Elkins went to the side of the coffin, stroked Cloudy's head and continued:

"I am now going to ask Seb Morris to say a few words about Mole's life."

Seb took a swig from a hip flask, as he walked up to the lectern.

"Mole enna got no proper family, so I a' bin asked by Jenny ter say a few words about 'im. 'E was around Earlsbrook when I was a boy, an' seemed like an old man ter me then! 'E never seemed ter age like most of we, the reason bein' 'e never 'ad a birthday, 'cause 'e didna know when 'e was born... so 'ow could 'e? I remembers when 'e used ter come spud-bashin' fer me dad - when the day's work was over 'e took more taters 'ome in 'is pockets than 'e'd put in the trailer; me dad always turned a blind eye."

Seb took another swig from the flask. "As I was sayin', Mole was a true countryman, born in the days when farmin' was 'arder than what it is now. Everythin' was done by 'and then; no newfangled machines like we 'ave terday, see? I never seen anyone cut a swede like 'im; 'e could 'ave one landin' in the trailer, one in the air, one in the hand, and another bugger in the ground, shiv'rin'!

"Mole was always better with animals than 'e was with yumans! 'E seemed ter understand 'em, an' they understood 'im; 'e could talk perfect 'orse, sheep and dog. If we 'ad a difficult birth goin' on, I'd a' rather seen Mole comin' in the shed than any vet. I remembers one autumn day 'e come in the cowshed and said: 'We're in fer an 'ard winter.' I says: "Ow d'yer work that out, Mole?' 'E says: "Cause o' the bloody 'orses.' So, I says: 'What about the 'orses?' An' 'e says: 'They've all growed thicker coats this autumn!' An' 'e was right: we 'ad more snow that winter than we'd 'ad fer years!

"Another time, me dad was showin' Mole his latest gadget: an incubator fer the chicken eggs. 'E showed 'im 'ow it turned the eggs automatic, like, an' 'ow it governed the temperamature an' 'umidity. Mole looked at 'im, sorta' sideways, an' says: 'What yer need all that fer, when a chicken can do it with its arse?' An', o' course, 'e wus right."

Seb turned to the vicar: "I'm sorry about the bad language, parson, but I'm a tellin' yer as it 'appened. I'd better shut up now: I knows yer got two more ter do today, but dunna fret: dead men canna complain."

He took another swig from his flask. "I knows that Jenny's gunna miss 'im more 'an anybody. 'E a' bin there all through 'er troubles, an' I know she'll miss 'im sleepin' in the cider 'ouse.

"Anyway, thank yer, and God bless yer, Mole."

As the bearers pushed Mole outside, into bright, autumn sunshine, eight jackdaws flew low over the congregation and settled along the apex of the chancel roof, like professional avian mourners. Reverend Elkin waited for people to gather round for the interment, and the bearers prepared to lower the coffin.

Cloudy walked between Jacob and Jenny, still carrying Mole's cap in his mouth. When they reached the graveside, Jenny stroked his head and offered her open palm to him. Doleful eyes studied her, then he dropped the cap into her hand and she placed it back onto the coffin. And, with that, Cloudy turned and ran, through the mourners and out of the lychgate.

As the coffin was lowered into place, the jackdaws lifted from the rooftop and disappeared, one by one, into the belltower.

*

When Jenny parked her truck in the yard at Poplar Farm, Jacob couldn't wait to see if Cloudy had returned. He ran over to the cider house, to find the loyal dog curled up asleep, on Mole's straw bale and hessian bags.

October, 2014

Jenny was picking mushrooms behind the barn, as her mind went over the events of Mole's funeral. The trees along the driveway to Poplar Farm were a blazing, yellow fire, as a low autumn sun rose behind them.

Eddie the postman swerved into the gateway, skidded to a halt and jumped out of his van. "More important post this morning, Jenny; looks real official, this one. If those are magic mushrooms you're picking, I'll expect to see you dancin' naked around the barn, on me way back from the village!" He handed her the envelope, slammed the door of his van and was gone before she could answer.

She sat down at the kitchen table and opened the letter.

> *Dear Miss Montfort,*
> **Re: Samuel Gillion, deceased.**
>
> *I am sorry I did not introduce myself at the funeral yesterday. I very much wished to meet you, but was asked by Samuel not to contact you until after he was buried.*
> *Samuel has been a client of mine for as long as I can remember. He always felt indebted to your father for befriending him, when all others derided and, sometimes cruelly, mocked him. He was aware of his*

shortcomings, but could do nothing to defend himself. As you no doubt know, your father acted as a shield for Samuel, which enabled him to live his life the way he wanted. I know they were very close and that you have continued caring for him since your father died.

As a result, he always wished to pass his property and possessions, inherited from his father and accumulated by him, to your family upon his death. His simplistic view of the world did not fit with today's complex rules regarding financial affairs and the tax system; in short, he regarded taxation as state theft. I was therefore instructed to deal with any estate and Inland Revenue matters after his death. As you may know, his rustic manner hid a shrewd and careful person, who spent a very small proportion of his earnings. He died a very wealthy man.

In the period since his death, I have applied for probate and started to wind up his financial affairs. All taxes, duties and debts will need to be settled. Once this has been done all properties and holdings in his name will be transferred to you and registered in your name.

I have noted that the rental from Samuel's agricultural holdings have not been increased for many years. When all matters have been settled, I suggest that we discuss this and increase rents in line with the Rent (Agriculture) Act 1976.

I would be glad if you can contact me, as I shall need to have verification of your identity and address to progress these matters. In the meantime, I enclose a list of assets and property which form part of the estate, together with a copy of Samuel's will.

Finally, any property or valuables left on your premises, and originally belonging to Samuel, were gifted to your father more than seven years ago, and these do not form part of his estate. Please find attached a full list of assets to be transferred.

Yours sincerely,
Glenys Smithson, Solicitor.

LIST OF ASSETS:

91-acre broad-leaf wood and forestry plantation, known as Sheepcratch Hill.

Court Farm, Earlsbrook. To include farmstead, outbuildings, lands, woodland, fishing and shooting rights. The whole amounting to 175 acres.

Cottage, garden and contents known as Cobtree Cottage, Earlsbrook.

Deposit accounts: £336,000.00

"Court Farm!   Court bloody Farm!   Sheepcratch Hill...
and, he never, ever said a bloody word that he owned them!
The clever old sod!"

Jenny sat staring at the letter, and realized why the
Dunhill-Smiths were living so well; this one, small piece of
paper answered the question that had always puzzled her
father.   Jenny read the line again, to ensure she wasn't
dreaming:

*"The rental from Samuel's agricultural holdings have not
been increased for many years..."*

"Well, it soon bloody well will be increased!" Jenny said
out loud, just as Jacob came into the kitchen.

"What are you talking about, Mum?"

Jenny hesitated before answering, and changed the
subject.

February, 2015

Jenny walked up the cottage path, between drifts of snowdrops and bud-laden daffodils. On the wall was a highly-polished brass plaque: *"Miss Glenys Smithson (Solicitor)."* Jenny tapped the equally-polished brass knocker. The door opened.

"Miss Smithson? Jenny Montfort. I hope I'm not too early."

"No; perfect timing: I've just put the kettle on. Please come in."

Jenny entered the low-ceilinged room, with piles of papers stacked on every available surface.

"Please sit down. I'm so pleased to meet you, after all these years. I have heard so much about you and your father, I feel as though I know you intimately, anyway. Samuel only came here about three or four times, in all the years that I've been dealing with his affairs. As you know, he was a man of few words, but the only words he ever had for you and your father were of the highest regard."

"How long have you known him?" Jenny asked.

"I first met him after his father died, when I dealt with his estate... so, that's more than forty years ago."

"Do you know why he never told us about all his property?"

"I don't think he told your father everything, in case it spoilt his relationship with him. I do know that they talked about his little stashes of rainy-day money: they agreed that the last man standing would leave things in order. One day, soon after your father died, he came out here on his bike, looking very agitated. He had an old, wooden shoe box tied to his cycle's carrier, bound up with baler twine. He came into this room, dumped the box on the table and said: 'You'd better sort this lot out, missus.' The rest is history, as they say."

"So, what was in the box?"

"Deeds, receipts, bank-books, keys, spiders, mouse-droppings and dust! Everything smelt of woodsmoke. It took me a day to sort out the important stuff. Regular cash payments went into the bank all his life, until they closed the local bank, three years ago; nothing seems to have gone anywhere since. I suppose there must be a stash of money, lying somewhere around Cobtree Cottage." At that, Miss Smithson pushed a bunch of heavy, old, steel keys across the table.

"Can you tell me what you know about Court Farm, and how he came to own it?" Jenny said.

"Inherited, through the generations; Samuel was the third, as far as I know. There are some gaps in the paperwork, but he has title to all of the lands I described. Once they are transferred to you, a rent review is a must. It will come as a shock to the current tenants, but they must have known that one day things would alter."

"How much have they been paying?"

"As far as I can tell, there has been no increase since before the current tenant took over from his father, and that was over twenty years ago. They pay eight-hundred pounds per annum in January, and that includes shooting rights on Sheepcratch Hill and fishing rights on the river."

"You cannot be serious! It's worth twenty times that!"

"Alas, I am serious. When I asked him, Samuel would not talk about it. Neither would he talk about taxes. Cash was all he knew about... and all he cared about. He told me that someone came to his house one day, from the Inland Revenue - when I asked him what happened, he said, and I quote: 'I acted bloody dull, and they went away and never came back.' I asked him if he had received any letters, and again, I quote: 'I canna read, so if a letter comes, I burns it.'"

"That sounds like the Mole I knew and loved. If only we could all do the same!"

"If you'd like me to provide you with the contact details of the Agricultural Fair Rents people, I'd be happy to do so. Once all this is registered to you, you can follow their guidance and get things up to date."

*

Jenny drove into the farmyard, feeling happier than she had ever been since that fateful day on Midnight Ridge. At last, she knew the truth about why the Dunhill-Smiths were so well off, and she was in a position to knock Phoebe off of the over-inflated cushion of ego that she sat on.

She got out of the truck and shouted over to Jacob, who was cleaning out the stable: "Come with me, son; I've got something to show you."

In the cider house, she swept hay from the floor, exposing the hiding place of the hoard. "What are you doing, Mum?" he asked, as she pulled the board from the floor.

"I'm not really sure, myself. But, you may get a surprise in a minute!"

She lifted the ammunition box from the hole. "Are you ready for this?" She flicked the catch open.

To her surprise, a thick, brown envelope lay on top of the hessian bags containing the coins, sealed by a red sealing-wax Tudor rose. She turned it over and gasped: her name was handwritten, in bold italics.

"What the...? We'd better take this in the house."

"What is it, Mum?" Jacob said, as he went to lift the box. "Wow, it's heavy! What's in it?"

"You'll see. Let's get it in the house, first."

As soon as Jacob placed the box on the kitchen table, he pulled out one of the bags.

"Coins! Gold coins! How did they get there? How did you know about them?"

Jenny stared at the envelope, her fingers reluctant to break the seal.

"Go on, Mum: open it; your name's on it."

Jenny slid the carving knife under the seal, slitting the envelope neatly open. The bundle of papers inside were yellowed with age and tied with a faded ribbon.

"What does it all mean, Mum?"

Jenny stared at the bundle of papers. "I don't believe it. I just don't believe it."

"Believe what, Mum?"

"I couldn't tell you before, but I've just seen a solicitor: Mole has left all of his property to us... which amounts to about half of Earlsbrook! These coins were his, and now they are ours, too."

"Wow! Does that mean we're rich?"

"Well, in some ways yes, and in some ways no."

"What do you mean?"

"It means that we own a lot of property and a lot of money... What we don't have is your dad, and we'd both be better off having him than all the property and money in the world."

There was a long silence, as Jacob took in the meaning of his mother's words. "I know what he looked like, from the photograph by your bed. But, do you know what I wish I could do?"

"No, darling. What?"

"Smell his skin and hear his voice."

Jenny turned away, to hide tear-filled eyes.

April, 2015

Jenny was reading through the solicitor's letter, which finalized Mole's estate. Also enclosed were the deeds to Sheepcratch Hill, Cobtree Cottage and Court Farm.

All three had been part of a huge estate, which was broken up and sold off, over many years. Court Farm came into the hands of the Gillion family in 1846, and Sheepcratch Hill was purchased by an Albert Gillion, in 1904 - Jenny assumed that this was Mole's grandfather. Cobtree Cottage had always been his home, but no one ever went there except him. Jenny could never remember her father visiting, or even talking about it.

Jacob came downstairs and piled a dish high with cereal. "Can we go to Mole's cottage today, like you said, Mum? We might find some more treasure."

"I doubt it, darling, but yes, we should go; I've been putting it off for too long."

*

Jenny parked by the gate. The cottage was surrounded by philbert bushes, damson trees and a high hawthorn hedge. From the road, it was more hermitage than home; the wicket gate was overgrown with brambles and nettles. Jenny got her father's billhook from the truck.

"This is great! Like cutting through a jungle," Jacob said, as his mother hacked her way into the garden.

As she opened it, one gate hinge fell off. Jacob ran ahead, through chest-high weeds.

The cottage was red brick, with a tumbled-down Victorian privy attached to the end, which looked as though it had been in regular use. A wellhead stood a few yards from the back door, with a bucket still hanging from the rope and winder. A pile of ashes nearly as high as Jacob was piled against the cottage wall, with a smaller pile of tea leaves beside it. Jenny fumbled through her bunch of keys and chose the largest.

"Can I go in first?" Jacob said, as the lock clicked open.

The tiny living room had a black, cast-iron range, which appeared to have been used until Mole's death. The room looked just as it would have done when his grandfather had lived there; nothing in the room belonged to the twentieth-first - or even the twentieth - century, apart from an old transistor radio. A single light socket, with no bulb in it, hung above a pine table, while numerous partly-burned candles stood on ledges and shelves around the room, dead matches lying beside each one. A chair beside the fireplace looked well used, with a pile of hessian sacks on a stool at the side.

"Wow, this is really spooky, Mum!" Jacob said, as he opened a door, leading to a rickety staircase. Jenny went up first.

"Oh, my god; what a mess! We can't go any further," Jenny said, as her eyes fell on the devastation. The ceiling had fallen down, onto what was left of a bed, and a gossamer curtain of cobwebs hung across the room, like part of a Hallowe'en film set.

"We'd better leave this for today, darling, and come back when we have more time. Go back down; it's not safe up here."

Jenny was just getting into the truck, when Phoebe

Dunhill-Smith came down the lane, on Pegasus. Jenny had not spoken to her since she had been to Court Farm and was snubbed by Henry, fourteen years earlier; neither had they spoken to her at Jacob's inquest.

She did not know that Jenny had become the legal owner of Court Farm, just a few days earlier, as she stopped and looked down from the saddle, at Jenny.

"Oh... hello, Jennifer. I'm sooo glad to have seen you; I think it's high time we were able to be civil to one another again. Don't you?" Each word was oiled with condescension.

Jenny could not believe that Phoebe would have the nerve to speak to her, after all that she had put her through. Jacob was already in the passenger seat, so she turned to face her.

"Yes, I agree. But, now is not the moment. You had your chances; now I shall choose the time, place and circumstances. But, trust me, you haven't got long to wait."

With that, Jenny slammed the truck door, started the engine and drove off, leaving Phoebe and Pegasus standing in a cloud of blue smoke.

Summer Solstice, 2015

A marquee stood on the lawn of Court Farm, in readiness for Phoebe Dunhill-Smith's fiftieth birthday celebration. Florists were arranging flowers, the barman was stocking shelves with wine, and staging was being erected for musicians. A refrigerated trailer purred beside the marquee, as a hog was being basted on a spit, nearby. Henry was fixing parking signs to gateposts, as Phoebe placed horseshoe name-cards on tables. Her sister was tying pink bows to the back of each chair.

Jenny was riding Trudy on Midnight Ridge, when she saw Seb Morris coming up the drover's road, on his tractor. He stopped by his sheep-cratch and switched off the engine.

"What's goin' on with that there big tent at Court Farm then, Jenny?"

"According to the village jungle drums, it's her fiftieth birthday party tonight. A big bash, I'm told."

"I'll bet you enna got an invite, 'ave yer, girl?" A wry smirk spread across Seb's face.

"No. Neither have any villagers, by the sound of it, Seb - even the people who've worked for them for years; it's a posh-knobs do only."

"'Untin', shootin' and fishin' brigade, I 'spect. Well you'm a hunter, so why don't yer just turn up?"

"Well, I had thought about it. I've got some legal papers for them to read, which they might find interesting."

"Like what?"

"Well, Seb, you've been a good friend and neighbour, and stuck with me through thick and thin, so you'll be the first to know: Mole was the mystery owner of Court Farm."

"Yer bloody jokin!"

"No, no; I'm very serious."

"'Ow come d'yer know that?'"

"His will; I had a letter, out of the blue. Most of Sheepcratch Hill - the woodland and pine plantation - all his as well."

"Well, I'll be buggered! I thought 'e'd die worth a bob or two, the crafty old sod, but... Never said a word ter me, in all the years I know'd him."

"I don't think my dad knew, either. It seems that Mole inherited as the last of the line, and couldn't handle it, so he threw the ball into his solicitor's court. God gave him very little to work with, so he lived his life the best he could and told no one. Anyway, now it's my problem: he's left everything to me, to be handed on to Jacob, when my time comes."

"Well, bloody 'ell! I'm really pleased for yer, girl. That means yer'll own all the ground around me now. What yer gunna do about the bloody Dunghill-Smiths, as I calls 'em?"

"Well, the first thing is to tell them that their rent is going up twenty-fold. They've been ripping Mole off for years, and I've spoken with the fair rents people - now, I've got to present them with the findings. Phoebe and Henry are not going to be happy."

"Well, I'll 'company yer, if yer wants ter do it, lass. Y'owes 'er one. I'd like ter see the smile wiped off 'er posh face – an' 'is: 'e's shot more pheasants on my land than I 'ave meself! Let's do it ternight, when all the knobs are there; 'ave a bit of a laff."

"I don't know if I could do that - as little as I like her or Henry."

"I'll take yer. Just turn up, like, out of the blue, give 'er the papers an' walk out."

Jenny had never felt vindictive in her life, but Seb's suggestion would not leave her thoughts, as she prepared Jacob's lunch. She recalled all the hours of misery she had endured after Jacob was killed, and the snub at Court Farm, when Phoebe would not see her. Then, her bare-faced cheek, approaching Jenny outside Mole's cottage. And, all this while they were living above their means, at Mole's expense.

She picked up the telephone.

"Hello, Seb. I've been thinking about what you said. Pick me up at seven o'clock; we'll do it!"

*

The weather forecast on the radio was of high pressure with sporadic thunderstorms, for the West Midlands and Welsh border. Jenny had hay bales standing in the field, which needed to come in before the rains came. Jacob and Jenny worked all afternoon, hauling and stacking the bales in the barn, and had just finished when Seb pulled into the yard, on his tractor.

"I thought we was goin' ter Court Farm."

"Sorry, Seb: I hadn't realized the time."

Jenny ran into the house, grabbed her envelope and left Jacob, bedding down the horses.

*

She sat on the tractor mudguard beside Seb, as they bounced

up the lane to Court Farm. The house, lawn and marquee glowed in a shaft of crepuscular sunlight, which lanced a storm-cloud to the west of Midnight Ridge. The only sign of life in the yard was Pegasus, looking out from his stable. They dismounted and walked around toward the marquee.

The smell of roast pork drifted on the evening air, as drinkers sat at tables on the manicured lawn. Jenny stood still, fingering the envelope and looking at the display of profligacy before them.

"Come on then, girl; I canna wait ter see 'er face."

"I don't know whether I can do it, now we're here."

"O' course yer can. All yer gotta do is walk through all the knobs, give her the papers an' walk out. Simple!"

Jenny looked at the envelope and saw Mole's toothless grin.

As she marched across the lawn, silence spread through the crowd, like water flooding dry sand. Glasses were placed back on tables, as glances, winks, nods and frowns swept across the sea of faces. All heads turned, following her progress, as Jenny reached the ornate drapes which lined the marquee and stopped by a milk churn, filled with an arrangement of lilies.

Henry had just mounted the stage to address the adoring party, while Phoebe stood in the centre of the dancefloor, awaiting an outpouring of praise about his wonderful wife - the silence which had enveloped the crowd only increased her expectation. Henry saw Jenny first. He stood in front of the microphone, open-mouthed, as Phoebe pouted a kiss at him. When Jenny pushed a chair aside, as she started toward the dancefloor, Henry's jaw hung like an open rat trap.

Phoebe breathed: "Don't be shy, daaarling."

Just as Jenny reached her, she turned, realizing that

something was amiss. Jenny was standing behind her on the plush, red carpet, her Wellington boots and green boiler suit covered in hay seeds and dried horse muck. She held out the envelope to Phoebe.

"Oh... Oooh, Jennifer, darling, how nice of you! What is it?"

"Do you *really* want to know, Phoebe, daaaarling?"

Phoebe had a look of utter panic in her eyes, but could not lose face in her finest moment.

"It's a rent increase for that farm of mine that you are living in - the first for twenty years. I wanted you to be the first to know, on this very special day!"

Emboldened, Jenny then jumped onto the stage and grabbed the microphone, as Henry stood speechless and helpless.

"I do hope you all have a wonderful evening; it may be your last chance, so make the most of it. Your hosts are about to start paying a fair rent for the farm, and I'd like you all to know that the luxury you enjoy tonight has been provided by the ruthless exploitation of a defenceless man, for over twenty years. Shall we all raise our glasses to Mole."

Jenny then took a glass of Champagne, standing on a table by Henry. "To Mole!" she said, lifting the glass high.

A ballooning silence hung over the bemused faces, until Rodney Forrester, the hunt whipper-in, stood and walked to the front of the stage, below Jenny. He turned to face the crowd and raised his glass: "To the memory of Mole."

The guests stood and raised their glasses to Mole. Phoebe ran from the marquee.

Jenny thrust the microphone at Henry and jumped down from the stage. Rodney walked back with her, to rejoin Seb.

"Well, that's told Mrs. Dunghill-Smith proper, Jenny, lass! She 'ave 'ad that comin' fer a long time," Seb said, his face red with excitement.

The air outside had changed from a balmy summer evening to a swirling storm. As Jenny and Seb walked across the lawn, a lightning bolt hit a pole carrying electricity to the farm, fusing the supply; the thunderclap which followed shook the buildings and ground they stood on.

As the tractor rattled out of the yard, in semi-darkness, the empty stable-door swung freely in the wind. Neither Phoebe nor Pegasus were anywhere to be seen.

Printed in Poland
by Amazon Fulfillment
Poland Sp. z o.o., Wrocław

53952095R00051